TORN

APHRODITE AND MESSIAH'S DILEMMA

A Novel by
RAE

To submit a manuscript for our review, email us at

submissions@majorkeypublishing.com

Be sure to LIKE our Major Key Publishing

page on Facebook!

Prologue

Aphrodite Samuels

"Aye, let's go to the park or something. Man, it's boring!" Haley, my best friend since diaper days, shouted as she jumped like a monkey on my bed. I stayed in a two-bedroom apartment with Haley near the University of Georgia, the school I was attending. It was pretty nice for the two of us, having enough room so that we wouldn't step on each other's toes.

I cut my eyes at her as I flipped through another page in my Psychology 101 book. Not even halfway through the course, I already had an exam. It was too fucking early for this shit! Haley was getting on my nerves. She kept bugging me and shit about going out. I kept telling her ass that I had to study, but no. She didn't want to listen. She was lucky I loved her. Any other bitch would've gotten these hands.

What are the biological factors that affect our behavior?

I quickly jotted down that question on my notepad before continuing to skim through the page.

"Aye, bitch. I know you hear me."

Your brain, nerves, and hormones are responsible for your thoughts, feelings, and actions. When you get

9

hungry, remember your favorite place to eat, smell food cooking, and take a big bite - biological processes are involved.

"Dite, baby, listen to me."

Ugh! Why wouldn't this girl shut up? I really needed to get through this chapter.

"Baby cakes? Boo thang? My ri—"

"Damn, child. What do you want?" I asked, frustrated. I needed to get my own apartment. I swear. I stared expectantly at my bubbly slender best friend as she giggled at my frustration. I swear, this child here...

"Nah, don't laugh now. Tell me what you want, girl. I need to study, and you know this."

She only rolled her eyes at me and kissed her teeth. Bitch.

"Well..."

She paused dramatically, making me want to throttle her.

"I was thinking we can go out, meet some boys, and live life. You know your ass stays cooped up in this apartment. Girl, you're only seventeen."

This heifer. I rolled my eyes. Haley was what you would call a freeloading friend. Now I'm not saying she didn't pay her fair share of the rent. She does, but that

10

was mainly because of her so-called sugar daddies. My best friend was a hoe, but at the end of the day, she had my back. The only fault she really had was her laziness. She didn't like to do anything! She didn't have a job. She spent her daddy's money. She didn't go to school. Shit, she barely graduated high school. Without me, she would've probably flunked. All she did was smoke, drink, and party. She failed to realize that unlike her, I had school to focus on.

I guess opposites did attract. For as long as I could remember, she had always been the wild child with an 'I don't give a fuck attitude', whereas I was easy going, yet hard working, doing everything necessary to brighten my future. My parents didn't raise me to be dependent. I was always told that if you don't work, you don't eat. Until this day, I still lived by the saying.

"Hales, you know I have an exam on Monday, which only gives me two days to study this material thoroughly. I can't stop and go places with you every time you bored. If my grades drop, you know my dad is going to be on my back until I pull them up. I ain't having that!"

I sighed, jotting down more notes. She only grunted before sitting down on my bed. I guess she got the message, finally!

11

Your nervous system is an interconnected network of nerve cells (called neurons) that allow you to sense the things going on around you so you can re-.

"Yonk!" Haley sang as she snatched my book from my hand.

"The fuck? Stop playing, Hales. Give it back!" I snapped angrily. She was so damn playful. It was annoying.

"Uh-uh. You, young lady, are coming with me. Now get dressed! And I don't want to hear another peep out of you! Don't make me come back in here!" she shouted over her shoulder as she sashayed out of the room like she was Naomi. I sucked my teeth. Well, I guess I had to go. Her ass wasn't going to leave me alone if I didn't. Man, I fucking hated her so much sometimes.

I hopped out of my bed and switched out of my sweats for a pair of black leggings, along with a red muscle shirt and my white Air Forces. I also grabbed my jean-like cross body bag that contained a notepad and pencil with my backup psychology book and phone before exiting my room. I'd go with her, but I wouldn't do anything, so I might as well study and take notes. Haley didn't know about my backup textbook.

12

"Ooh, I see you with your cute self," Haley gushed as she eyed my attire as I did hers. She was dressed in a blue mid-thigh T-shirt dress, along with a pair of nude Toms and a Tommy Hilfiger bucket hat. Look at my best friend, looking all cute and things. I smirked as I gazed at Haley. This girl was always dressing to the ten no matter where she went. She could be going to the grocery store and would still be all dolled up. I mean, I guess she had the time, considering, so yeah.

"Let's go, child."

***

Two chapters down and two more to go. I sighed and stared at the first page of chapter three, sensation and perception. I huffed before taking a sip from my Zephyrhills water bottle. I sat on a picnic bench that was next to a basketball court where sweaty college dudes played street basketball from time to time. Haley being Haley had already scurried out to meet her next prey as she liked to call them. I swear my best friend could be such a hoe at times, but who was I to judge. After all, she was my best friend, and I ought to love her.

I absentmindedly gazed at the small writing, feeling overwhelmed with boredom. Lord Jesus, this crap was so confusing! I'd have to go over this yet again when I got back home.

"Intro to sensation and perception," I read out loud in a monotone voice. Fuck, man! Maybe I should take a break.

"Aye, watch out!"

Before I could react, I was hit in the face with a ball. The force was strong enough to knock me off of my seat. I groaned. Who the hell? I rubbed my nose and growled. Dumb ass niggas needed to watch where they threw shit! That thing had hit me straight in the face. I swear these people out here were trying to give me a concussion or something.

"Aye, you alright? My bad, lil' mama," I heard some dude say before his face came into view. Damn, I thought. This boy had been blessed. He had some pretty green eyes that seemed to sear into my soul as we gazed at each other. Those lips, man, I wonder what kind of tricks he could do with his mouth pi——. Wait, no. You're a virgin, Dite. Calm down.

I quickly snapped back into reality and glared at his pretty ass.

14

"Your fuck ass threw that shit? Nigga, you almost gave me a concussion!" I shouted. This fool had the audacity to laugh at me. Ugh! The nerve!

"You know what? I will press charges. Yep! Move!" I snapped as I rose to my feet, pushing him away in the process.

"Ruining my mood and shit," I mumbled, dusting off the back of my shorts.

"For real, though, I'm sorry. We didn't mean to hit you. My boys and I were just playing some ball. My bad. You need some help with that?" this cheeky bastard had the nerve to ask as he looked at my backside. Lord Jesus, please take the wheel!

"No thank you, but I will need your name when I call the police," I lied. I wasn't going to call the cops. I mean, why would I? It wasn't that serious, but I wouldn't mind getting his name though. Maybe I'd get his numb——. No, Dite. It's all about school. School! School! School!

"Oh okay. I peeped that. Messiah Arius Zahir Lafayette is the name. And yours, beautiful?"

I rolled my eyes. He thought he was cute.

"Aphrodite Aasiyah Khepri Samuels. Thank you kindly, Mr. Lafayette, for knocking me on my ass and fucking up my study time."

15

I fumed as I gathered my things off of the table.

"Well, ass wipe, have a nice day! My people will call your people."

With that said, I left. Mr. Lafayette stayed on my mind ever since that day. After that, we started kicking it. He became my best male friend in college and maybe, just maybe, a bit more.

Aphrodite Samuels

Fuck! I groaned, feeling tired as shit. I had just gotten back from track practice, and now I had to change and head to the library for my tutoring session with some twelfth grader that went to the local high school around here. I tutored in English part-time since it was always my strongest subject in school. Plus, I needed the extra cash. It had been about a year and some change since I'd been enrolled at the University of Georgia. Haley and I still stayed in the same apartment, and things had been cool so far. Messiah and I were like two home skillet biscuits, but I couldn't lie and say that was all that we were. I low key had the tiniest crush on him, and it didn't help that he loved on me like we were together. I mean, I guess I wanted more, but I don't know. It was complicated.

Sighing, I shrugged out of my thoughts and allowed my gym bag to drop to the floor. It made a loud thumping sound when the bottom of the bag collided with the floor. I kicked off my shoes as well before heading straight for my bedroom.

I ignored the faint moans that came from Haley's room and shrugged. She was probably fucking some random that she'd met at the store or something. Since

17

she didn't go to school and couldn't keep a job, all she did was sleep around. I wasn't gon' judge her. What she did in her spare time was none of my business.

As soon as I as I got to my room, I hopped in the shower. I wasn't about to go anywhere smelling like all my life I had to fight. Nope, not I. After a good twenty-minute shower, I had gotten dressed before preparing my tutoring bag. I dropped in the notepad with the key points that I had to discuss with Charlie, my student, as well as a few pens, highlighters, note cards, and such. I then checked the timing on my phone. I was supposed to meet the kid around five. It read 4:40. It only took me ten minutes to get to the campus library by car without traffic. Today was a pretty peaceful day, and traffic was good, so I would be good.

I slung my bag over my shoulder before leaving my room. The sounds of moans I heard before were now replaced by giggles. Well, this was new. Haley usually kicked her flings out after sex. I chuckled lightly. I guess someone had finally tamed miss no love. As I grew closer to the main part of the house, the giggling became more apparent. It was coming from the living room. I smirked. Nah, he was just leaving.

"You going to come back later?" I heard her ask hopefully, making me retract my earlier statement. Could this be? Had my little Haley actually caught feelings?

"I don't know, man. Bambie and I had some things planned after she finished her session. I mean, I might."

I froze at the sound of the name Bambie. Nobody called me that, but...

"Messiah!"

Oh, fuck nah! Are you fucking serious, bruh? Where the fuck was Ashton? Somebody must have been trying to prank my ass. I know my two best friends were not hooking up. I looked at Haley with an 'explain yourself' look and then to Messiah in disbelief. I needed some answers, and I needed them now.

"Hey, Dite! When did you get in?" Haley asked in an innocent tone. I mugged her. If looks could kill this heifer would be casket ready.

"Never mind that. What's going on here?" I asked, gesturing between the two, if that was even possible. There was like zero space between these two. A pang of jealousy struck me in the pit of stomach as I scrutinized the two. The rational part of me already knew what was going on, but the heartbroken side needed it to be voiced.

"Uh, well we're kind of together. Isn't that good?"

This heifer.

*"So you mean to tell me you and Haley are together?"
I asked in disbelief. How dare this bitch and this nigga
stand in my face and say that shit to me! Her ass was
smirking like she was the shit with his hand in hers. Oh,
this hoe! I closed my eyes and sighed. He ain't your man,
Dite. With that thought in mind, I mustered up a fake ass
smile for their asses.*

*"Well, congratulations. I guess. I am about to head to
the library. I'll see you when I see you."*

*I quickly slung my cross bag over my chest and left
their grimy asses in the apartment. Fuck it! I mean, how
the hell was she going to tell me to go for Siah, knowing
that I liked him, but dig her dirty ass claws into him
instead? His ass wasn't any better. I couldn't believe his
ass had the audacity to have me spread out all over his
bed, up under him and shit, being balls deep inside a
bitch, but then he went to go fuck with my best friend.
That shit was foul as fuck, bruh, but it was cool. It was
cool. I would keep calm.*

*That's who he really wanted, just an easy hoe. That
wasn't me. She could have him. Stop that, Dite! She's
your best friend. Don't let a nigga come between eighteen
years of a friendship. Sighing, I ran my right hand*

20

through my large curly fro. I really couldn't even be mad
though. We were not together. Plus, I had never told him
how I felt, so it's not like he knew. I guess he thought we
were just fucking. You know what? It was whatever. I had
to just let him go. Let Messiah do Messiah.

CHAPTER 1

Aphrodite Samuels

"Listen up, little ones! Jamie here has an announcement. Go ahead!"

I gestured, kneeling down to the small five-year-old's height and gave him a little push, encouraging him to make his announcement. I watched him blush a little before speaking.

"Well, my birthday is on Saturday, and everyone is invited!"

He cheered happily, earning a cheer from the rest of the class. Jamie grinned as he handed out each of his invitations to his classmates.

"Spiderman!" Carlos, another one of my students, cried in excitement upon receiving his invite. I laughed and watched happily as everyone began to talk about his party and all the cake and ice cream they were going to receive. It warmed my heart to see all these innocent faces every day. It made me wish that I had a child of my own. I knew that I was in no rush. I was only twenty-five, so it wasn't like my time was ticking. Plus, I hadn't really found the one. Well, I did, but that was just a distant memory that I longed for deep down. Everyone who knew of my still existing love for this man had told me to

22

forget him, but it was hard to forget your first love. I had tried to get over it, but it just wouldn't stop!

I felt a tug on my pants leg that brought me out of my thoughts. I looked down to see Jamie's big hazel brown eyes looking up at me with a cute shy smile on his face, showcasing his left cheek dimple. I smiled and opened my mouth.

"Yes, baby?" I asked, noticing his left hand was behind his back. I gazed at him in confusion but shrugged. He used his free hand to gesture for me to squat down to his level. I complied and shrunk down to his height.

"U-uh, Miss Sam, my mommy said I could invite all my friends..." he trailed off as his left hand came from behind his back, revealing cardboard cutout of a cupcake. It had pink frosting, colorful buttons, and gems for decorations with "Miss Sam" printed on the body of the cupcake.

"Mommy helped me make this for you. Will you please come to my party, Miss Sam?" he asked cutely in a nervous tone. Well, who could say no to a face like that?

"Ah, thank you, munchkin! I would love to come to your party. I wouldn't miss it for anything in the world."

I happily took the invitation from him, giving him a huge hug with a smile.

"Miss Sam is coming to my party!" he screamed bashfully before he ran off to join the others in their discussions about his party as they colored a bit.

I loved teaching little kids. I used to take early childhood development back when I was in high school for dual enrollment. I was already certified to be a preschool teacher, so I decided to major in elementary education and minor in child psychology. I felt so much pride and joy in the fact that I could help enrich the youth who may someday enrich our society. I sighed happily. I loved my job.

***

"How many times do I have to tell you we are done?"

"Man, why are you tripping? We can work this out!"

I rolled my eyes at the voice of my ex, Omar, as he pleaded with me for us to get back together. Besides Messiah, he was another reason I didn't do relationships. He was so controlling, clingy, whiny, and annoying. He was also childish, and it was not cute for a twenty-seven-year-old to act like a child. He would always think I was keeping secrets from him. Turns out, he was the one with the dirty laundry.

24

Two years into our relationship, I found out that not only did he have two kids, but he also had an ex-wife. Now I didn't have a problem with him having his life before me, but that was a huge secret he kept from me. How you can say you love me and want to marry me but never mention your kids and ex?

He would also think I was cheating on him if I wasn't with him. He would be like "don't be having another nigga in your house" or "tell that nigga you over there giggling with I said hey!" He was straight up sounding like an emotional insecure ass female. I didn't take relationships lightly when it came to love. If I loved you, it meant you had all of me. I didn't do cheating. Tamar, my mother, did that to my dad. I saw how much that hurt him, so I would never wish that upon anyone else.

"Boy, work what out? You were the one with all the accusations and secrets. It was you who ruined our relationship!"

I fumed, annoyed. I could hear him suck his teeth in aggravation. I placed my Galaxy S6 between my ear and shoulder as I held my bags while unlocking the door to my house. I stayed in a nice one-bedroom, one-bathroom apartment here in Atlanta. It wasn't anything extravagant, but I kept my place nice.

"Please, Dee. I'm begging you. Just give me one more chance. I promise I'll do right by you this time."

It was my turn to suck my teeth as I heard the lies spill out of his mouth. Lord Jesus, help me now! I prayed for my sanity. I couldn't believe anything this fool was saying. He had dogged me so many times in the past and said the exact same words as an apology. Being that I loved this kid, I continued to stay with his ass, but once I learned of his secret life, I'd had enough.

"Boy, no!"

"Oh, so you got a new nigga now? Is that I——?"

Without letting him finish that sentence, I hung up the phone. The nerve of that fool to call me a cheater!

I stepped out of my moccasins, shook my head, locked my phone, and rolled my eyes. So childish! He knew damn well I wasn't cheating on him. He was the one going behind my back with his ex. I couldn't believe that shit, but once my girl, Samantha, showed me the proof by taking me to ol' girl's house and allowing me to see them all booed up, looking like a happy family with their kids, I decided I needed to free myself of this insecure cheating ass motherfucker.

Apparently, he and his ex were trying to work things out for the sake of their kids. I mean, I wasn't gon' knock

26

you for trying to do what was best for you and yours, but don't bring me into your mess. I wasn't about that cheating thing, and for him to accuse me of the shit he did befuddled me. Omar was just another man I had come across that wanted to have his cake and be able to eat it too, but that was okay. I was going to keep my peace. He was old enough to know what he wanted. That wasn't me, so it was all good. I wasn't going to fight for a man who didn't want me to.

I sighed. *Man, I need my glass of Chardonnay,* I thought. I headed to the kitchen and pulled out a wine glass from my China cabinet before going into my freezer to get a bottle of Nay. I took my glass and cup to my bedroom and placed the bag with my school papers onto the bed. I decided to switch on Pandora as I sipped my wine and graded some papers. *Let's hear what my girl Ravaughn has to say today,* I thought as I skipped over Drake's station and spotted her station. "Best friend" by Ravaughn came on, and as I listened to the lyrics of the song, I could not believe what I was hearing.

If you open your eyes

And give sense a good try

I'll be all you need

And more

Than a fuckin' best friend

Really? I thought. *The story of my third wheel motherfucking life between Messiah, Haley, and I.* I rolled my eyes. *Really, Ravaughn? Really,* I thought again. I remembered all the times I would always play the third wheel whenever we all would go out. It would be like every time I made plans with Haley, Messiah would have to join, and every time I would make plans with Messiah, Haley would bounce her ass on over. I could not be with either one without the other. That shit was mad disrespectful. Haley knew how I felt for Messiah, and she still threw their relationship in my face.

I knew both of them knew how uncomfortable and awkward I felt being the single one in the group, yet they still continued to ease on down the road without a care in the world. Not only that, it always seemed like everyone knew about me and Messiah's business. Some would wonder why he was now with Haley. Others would say he played both of us. It was so embarrassing, but like I said, they didn't seem to care.

What Haley and Messiah had done was trifling as fuck. How could you go from telling me to go for the man of my dreams to fucking him instead? And how could you go from fucking and loving me to my best

28

friend? I didn't get it then, and I still didn't get it now. Maybe I needed to put it on some twerk music or something. I did not feel like being all up in my feelings right now. Sighing, I grabbed my phone and switched to Rich Homie Quan's station on my list. As soon as I switched stations, "Flex" blasted through my speakerphone. I nodded my head to the beat and got to work on those papers.

***

Being that I taught kindergarten, I managed to get through the grading process quickly. All I needed to do was place them in the grade book. I also downed two glasses of Chardonnay before calling it a night. Since it was Friday, I had an off day tomorrow, and I would also be attending Jamie's sixth birthday party. *Yay for Saturday*! I chuckled lightly and placed my glass on my nightstand table next to the Chardonnay bottle.

"Enough of you, Quan," I spoke, switching off Pandora before placing my phone on my charger.

"Time for bed, Dite," I said to myself as I placed my currently wavy hair into a bun. I stripped down to my underwear and made my way into the bathroom. There, I finished stripping and hopped into the shower. After washing, I put on my boy shorts along with an oversized

29

black tee and matching socks to go with it after I applied baby lotion to my body. The last I remembered was climbing back into bed and blacking out.

CHAPTER 2

<u>Aphrodite Samuels</u>

"Aye yo, Aphro! Wake your ass up, child!"

I groaned at the sound of my best friend. Samantha's, voice as she continued to attack me with a pillow. *How did this heifer get in?* I sat up, shooting her a questioning glare while yawning in the process.

"What you doing here?" I finally asked. analyzing her in confusion. I know this heifer hadn't hopped through my window. I lived on the second floor. so how the fuck? My eyes widened in realization when I remembered I had given her my spare key, which I specifically told her to use for emergencies only. I'd been wondering why every time I come home from work. it looked like my juice had been drunk and my bed had been laid in. I shook my head at her and rolled my eyes.

"You owe me a bottle of Chardonnay. You thought you were slick. coming into my house and drinking my juice while I was at work. Nah. homie. You lost your mind! What time is it?" I questioned, fixing my bun. I tended to shift a lot in my sleep, so I guess my hair tie had loosened.

Sam gave off a fake "bitch you thought" laugh as she checked the time on her HTC touch.

"It's 7:30. Why?"

Ignoring her question, I hopped out of bed and went into my bag, getting out the gift I had bought for Jamie after work. It was the Super Stadium Baseball Game. I remember back when I first started teaching his class at Hope Academy, I had my students introduce themselves to me and the class by telling us about their likes and dislikes, among other things. Jamie had mentioned he liked baseball, so I thought this gift was perfect for him.

"Hey, do you mind wrapping this for me?" I asked but more like demanded Samantha to do.

"I think I have some wrapping paper around here. Look in my desk drawer," I added without giving her a chance to speak. I could tell she was annoyed with me by the smacking sound she made.

"Bitch got me working on a Saturday," I heard her mumble. *Bitch should've never come here.* I inwardly laughed as I went into my closet. After a few minutes of pondering, I picked out a burnt orange colored bodysuit along with a pair of mom jeans. I placed the outfit on my bed along with my Calvin Klein undies before making my way into the bathroom. Switching on the water, I maneuvered the handles so that the temperature was right and hopped straight in.

32

After a good thirty-minute shower, I moisturized my body and got dressed. I also noticed that Samantha wasn't in my room anymore, but Jamie's gift was wrapped. Shrugging, I then slipped on a pair of Arizona sandals before applying nude gloss to my lips. I smiled to myself. *Don't I look good*, I mused as I assessed my attire in my standing, full-length mirror that sat along the wall on the right side of my bed.

"Yass girl! Lesbihonest. Now if only I swung that way," I joked to myself. Damn, I was looking good. I felt like Beyoncé. I was feeling myself. I laughed once more and rolled my eyes at my own childishness. *Let me get my tail out of here before I start using my bedroom voice on my reflection. Lord knows there's no going back from that.* With that in mind, I grabbed my clear Aviator glasses, phone, keys, and Jamie's gift before heading out.

As I got closer and closer to the living room, I could hear "Check" by Young Thug as well as the voice of my dear friend.

"Got me a check. I got a check. Oh, she was in my nigga DM trying to flex. When I see her, I might crack her fucking neck."

She sang the Sonyae remix to this song. I rolled my eyes once she came into view. Her ass was just chilling
33

and watching music choice from my forty-inch flat screen as she sipped some of my Nay and ate my Oreos. *Lord. please give me the strength.*

"Well don't you look comfortable," I stated in a sarcastic tone, earning a shrug from Sam before she looked at me.

"Where are you going, missy?" she asked before placing another mini Oreo into her mouth. The nerve! I mugged and ignored her question, giving her the finger as well.

"I'll be back!" I shouted over my shoulder, walking out of the door. I lived on the second floor of the building, so as soon as I was out of my apartment, I headed to the elevator. Once I made it to the first floor I quickly exited the building. Once I found my all-black Camry in the parking lot, I placed the gift and my bag in the back and hopped into the driver's seat. I switched on 95.3 and made sure to put on my seatbelt before cranking up my car and pulling off.

***

"Hey, Miss Sam!" the small child greeted, his eyes glazing with joy as he spotted the gift in my hand. His mother, Deshawn, smiled as she took the gift from me.

34

"So you're the one who has my son's nose wide open," she joked, making Jamie blush. I always knew Jamie had a small crush on me. I thought it was cute.

"Well he is a good student. Plus, he's my little helper. I enjoy having him in my class," I spoke sincerely, making my way into the living room. Their home was filled with boisterous little people running around as well as parents. I recognized some adults from "meet the teachers" night the day before school started back in August, and I saw some new faces as well.

"I'm glad to hear that. Let me put this up! I'll be back," Deshawn chirped, whisking the gift away.

"Miss Sam, come meet my friends," Jamie demanded, pulling my hand toward a group of kids that I didn't know.

"Guys, this is Miss Sam. Miss Sam these are my other friends; Anthony, Drake, Khalid, and Monte!"

He gestured toward each individual.

"So you his girlfriend? Dang! How you cuffed that, Jay?" Monte, I believe, said. *The fuck? So people just out here claiming me now? They don't ask or nothing.* I shook my head and playfully glared down at the little boy who remained by my side while he played with his fingers nervously.

35

"Oh, so I'm your girl now?" I asked, laughing.

"Well, see what had happened was..." he trailed off, trying to come up with a lie.

"Wait, so you ain't his girl? Well, how about you and I go somewhere quiet. 'Cause girl, I got a secret place that we can go 'cause I really want to be alone."

Oh my God. I couldn't help but laugh as I was being serenaded by a six-year-old. He was really feeling himself too. Grabbing my hands and caressing them as he sang each note. I could tell little Jamie was getting mad by the way he clenched his fist and glared at his friend.

"Leave that woman alone!" I heard a female shout, coming into the room. I immediately recognized the voice as Jamie's mom.

"But ma—"

"Miss C—"

"Nope, bye! Go outside and play. Gon' now."

She shooed all the boys. Little pouts formed on their faces as they trudged out of the house. I could've sworn Monte gave her that look as he passed her. I shook my head. *Kids*.

"I'm sorry about that. Let me introduce you to some people."

I nodded and let her do as she pleased.

36

Fuck, man. I have to pee. I shouldn't have drank all that tea. It was now almost one. I'd pretty much gotten acquainted with everyone here, including the kids who seemed to be taking quite the liking to me. Monte and Jamie were about ready to fight over who got to sit next to me when it was cake time. I was just laughing on the inside at their cuteness. The food was really good, man, I swear. The ribs? Oh them ribs, they were finger licking good. They'd make you want to smack your mama good. Deshawn also made some sweet tea, and everyone who knows me knows I loved me some iced sweet tea. Don't let me get started on that potato salad Jamie's grandmother, Miss April, made. That woman put her foot in that. I was going to need to get a to-go plate when I left.

The kids were currently outside in the bouncy house, playing on the slip and slide, or dancing. It was so adorable.

"Mmm. Chill, I know you got to pee. Her ass over there doing the pee, pee dance. Lord Jesus, let me get this baby to the bathroom before something happens!" Miss Kathy joked, making all the adults in the room laugh. I blushed a little. I was already about the youngest adult in

37

the room. What she said was just embarrassing. Hopping up, I allowed her to lead me to the bathroom.

"Okay now, chil'. All you gotta do is go up the stairs, and go down the hallway. The bathroom door is the second one on the right. You hear?"

I nodded and followed her instructions. I finally made it to the bathroom and sighed in relief as I hurriedly opened the door. I did my business and then washed my hands.

Bitch better have my money

Bitch better have my money

Bitch better have my, bitch better have my...

My pocket vibrated as Rihanna's voice blared. Without really looking at the caller I.D., I swiped the green tab to the right before placing the phone to my ear.

"Hello, this is Aphrodite Samuels speaking. How may I help you?" I chirped politely into the phone. Daddy said it was always best to answer your phone politely because you'd never know who might be calling you. It sounded strange, being that there was this thing called caller I.D., but I didn't question him.

"Girl, if you don't! You better gon' somewhere with that proper ass talk. I know you know who was calling you, talking about 'how may I help you'."

Why did people feel the need to clown me on a how I chose to speak? Was it a crime that I knew proper English or that Avery Samuels taught me right? I don't think so.

"Whatever. Why did you call me?" I asked as I squirted some hand sanitizer into my palms.

"You out of mini Oreos, and I also polished off the last of your pizza rolls."

This heifer. I clicked the end button, hanging up on her ass before rubbing the remaining sanitizer into my hands. She had some nerve.

I rolled my eyes at my reflection before exiting the bathroom. I didn't pay attention to my surroundings as I continued to stare down at my phone. I had thirty notifications; fifteen from Instagram, five from Twitter, and the rest were emails. I should've taken a mirror selfie. Nah, let me stop. Today was not about me. I was brought out of my thoughts as my body collided with another. Hands reached out to grab me so that I wouldn't fall.

"Oh shit! My ba— Bambie?"

"Binky?"

CHAPTER 3

Messiah Lafayette

"Binky?"

Damn. Lord have mercy on my soul. Dite looked hella different from when I last saw her. That was like what four years ago. It felt longer, but damn did time do the girl's body good, and I saw that she had lost a little baby fat. That ass still was thick though! Her hair had grown now. That shit fell down to the tip of her ass, and it was wavy. Jesus, her lips though, they were still juicy as ever, and don't let me get started on her eyes... long ass lashes. She was still my little Bambie, but damn did Bambie grow up!

Wait a minute, did she just call me Binky? Ah hell no! She knew damn well I didn't like that nickname. That shit didn't even sound right. Binky? Did I look like that little elephant bear thing from Arthur? She was still on that fufu shit. I swear.

Her curves feel so right, I thought, low key feeling her up. Damn, she smelled so good, baby lotion. She loved that shit and still did, I see. *Nigga, ain't you getting married?* Oh shit! I did have a girl, but I couldn't lie, because Bambie had a nigga feeling some type of way.

"Bambie. Shit. Damn!" I found myself saying in shock, taking her all in. *I see that ass is still plump,* I thought as I brushed my hand against it out of habit. Wait. I was getting married. Plus, she didn't want me. She wanted more than me. I guess she was just too good for me.

"You and that damn nickname!" her sexy yet raspy voice replied as she rolled her eyes. Damn. I loved that girl. Shit! Just hearing her voice had me missing the times when she used to scream out my name when we had sex, hitting all types of high notes and shit when a nigga was deep up in it. Wait. What the hell was she doing here?

"Girl, don't give me that. You know damn well you loved that name." I joked, playing off my anger and confusion. She still had that effect on me, but I couldn't love her. I didn't! I had my girl. Haley may not have been my first choice, but I did have love for the girl. I just wasn't sure if I was in love with her. Yeah, I proposed, but that didn't mean shit. She had just been my rider for some time. Plus, she always whined about putting a ring on it, acting like she was Beyoncé or some shit. So to satisfy her, I bought a ring.

"Yeah, well, that was then."

She paused and rolled her eyes, making me want to smack them out of her head. I had told her about that. She knew I hated when she rolled her eyes at me. That turned me on but also irritated the fuck out of me! Her ass looked so damn sexy as she slightly mugged me. I chuckled lightly. She must've forgotten who I was.

"You better stop rolling them eyes, girl!" I snapped, half playfully. All she did was smirk and kiss her teeth.

"Anyway, it was... um... nice to see you again. I got to go."

With that said, she eased on past me.

"Bye, Binky!"

There she went with that damn nickname again! *But God, that ass though.* I knew she knew what she was doing too, moving that ass like that. *Lord Jesus, pray for me.*

Aphrodite Samuels

"Bye, Binky!" I called over my shoulder as I eased on past him while trying to make sure our bodies didn't touch. My hormones were already racing at just the scent of him. Lord knows how long I had left until it became ungodly up in here. Knowing he was staring at my retreating figure, I managed to put a little extra sway in my hips. Messiah did always have a thing for my ass. I smirked. That boy thought that he was slick, low key feeling my ass and shit.

Although, I seemed cool then, I was actually freaking out on the inside. What the hell was he doing here? I distinctly remembered him telling me he was moving out of state after graduation. *Did he move back? Are him and Haley still together?* All these questions formed in my mind. I sighed, feeling sexually frustrated at the thought of him. *I need me a drink.*

CHAPTER 4

<u>Aphrodite Samuels</u>

After the encounter with Messiah, I made up an excuse to leave early. Jamie was a bit upset, but I told him I'd bring him cupcakes next week to make up for me leaving. I also didn't really see much of Messiah after that either. Come to find out, he was related to Jamie. Small world. I guess he had left or something. I shrugged. That was two weeks ago, so I didn't really care anymore. Let me stop lying. I was still freaking out about seeing him after all these years. The way he looked the other day and how he made me feel was unreal. I knew I shouldn't want him, but it was like my heart was saying otherwise.

I sighed. *Damn you, Messiah*! Anyway, it was Friday, and I had just come from work, so I decided to hit up Starbucks. I had to put the grades in the progress book, so what better place to do it than at Starbucks?

I was also in the mood for some of their delicious cinnamon chai tea lattes along with a brownie or two. Lord knows I loved me some Starbucks. If only I could I would marry it, but sadly, I couldn't. I sighed. We could all dream, right?

As I opened the door to the café, the smell of freshly brewed coffee filled my nostrils. I gazed around in pure

44

bliss as I looked at all the goodies. *Lord Jesus, I love me some Starbucks. Maybe I should get a chicken BLT too.*

"Good afternoon, ma'am. How may I help you?" greeted a tall slender blue-eyed brunette from behind the counter with a polite smile on her face. I smiled back and recited my order to the girl.

"Can I get a large cinnamon chai tea latte along with two brownies?"

"Will that be all?"

"Yes, thank you."

"Alright, your total is $10.25."

I handed her a twenty and waited for my change. She handed me $9.75 in return. She thanked me and told me to have a nice day, and I did the same. I waited patiently for the deliciousness as the woman continued to work. Not even moments later, my order was ready. I grabbed my treats and found an empty table to sit at.

After I got myself situated, I took out my laptop from my bag and opened it up so that I could log in to progress book. As soon as I finished that, I got the rest of my things out and started putting the assignment grades for the papers I had already finished into the system.

***

"Let's see what I got in here."

45

I opened the fridge to find a couple of V8 juices in there, some fruit, an opened box of Fruity Pebbles, and some milk. Sighing, I opened the top portion of my fridge and pulled out some shrimp. I knew I had some linguine somewhere around this bitch, so I decided to make shrimp scampi and linguine.

I grabbed a pot out of one of the cupboards and put some water and salt in it to boil. After a good little minute, I added the pasta to the boiling water. As that cooked, I whipped out a skillet and started on my shrimp sauce. I heated some butter and olive oil before placing some chopped garlic and crushed pepper flakes into it and let that cook for a bit. After a while, I added the rest of the ingredients and allowed the sauce to cook as I drained the pasta. I finished off the meal by dumping the pasta into the sauce and allowing it to cook.

"Chef Dite with the pot," I rapped, mimicking Drake in "0 to 100." I smirked at my masterpiece.

I happily served myself a healthy portion and grabbed a cold banana and strawberry V8 juice out of the fridge before chowing down. After eating, I took a quick shower and slipped into a pair of black and yellow Batman shorts and an all-black tee after I moisturized my body and put on my undies. That hot water kind of woke me up a bit, so I decided to hop on the gram for a while. I had forty follower requests. I accepted each one I passed. As I continued to scroll, I noticed that Messiah followed me as well. I clicked on his name and was greeted by all of his sexiness. *Two, four, six pack.*

I couldn't help but drool at the sight of his after workout figure. His abs glistened with sweat, making my lady parts cry out in need. *Boy, don't I sound parched?* I shook my head at myself but continued to gawk at his photos. Not once did I see him with a picture of a female, unless it was of him and the women in his family. Deep down, I was smiling at that. Maybe he and Haley had broken up. Maybe I had a chance now. I shook my head at myself. *What is wrong with me? He never wanted you, Dite. Haley was always what he wanted.*

He had just used me to get to her. I didn't know whether I wanted to cry or get angry at the thought. I couldn't believe I was still pining for this man after all these years, nor could I believe that he played me. That boy had my heart in the palm of his hand, and he played it. I shook my head. Look at me, sounding like Adele. I sighed. *Man, I'm stressing. I need me a cig.* Let me stop. I don't even smoke.

I rolled my eyes. Let me take my ass to sleep. I locked my phone and placed it on the charger before lying down and letting sleep consume me.

***

In the middle of the night, my phone rang. Bitch better have my money was blasting out loud and making it hard for me to sleep. I groaned. *Ri Ri shut your ass up*! *Oh my Lord. Can't anybody get any sleep around here*? I growled and snatched my phone off the nightstand. It was fucking two in the morning! My phone screen showed an unknown number, making me frown. Who the hell? Clearing my throat, I mustered up a professional voice before answering my phone.

"Hello, this is Aphrodite Samuels speaking. How may I help you?"

I was being way too chipper for it being this time in the morning. These people would get murdered, man. I swear.

"Hey, it's me. I have been trying to reach you since earlier, but I could never get through."

Who the fuck is me?

"Yeah, I'm going to need you to be more specific. Who exactly is me?" I asked, annoyed. I know God did not intend for me to be up at this godforsaken time. Jesus, please take the wheel because of the way I feel right now.

"Um, Haley. It's Haley. How are you doing, Dite?"

Ain't this about a bitch? First Messiah. Now her? I just can't get a break!

Something was telling me something wasn't right in the water.

"Hey, Hales! I'm fine. Why did you call me?" I asked curiously. I did not feel like beating around the bush. It was too early for that. Plus, I wanted to hear what she had to say.

"Uh, I'm sorry for calling you out of the blue, but I was wondering since I'm in town, could we meet up? I have some things to tell you."

She giggled, making me roll my eyes.

"Where are you?" I questioned.

"Oh, we've actually moved back down here." her ass gushed excitingly, almost gloating. *We?*

"Um, yeah. Sure. When would you like to get together?" I questioned. *Please do not let it be anytime soon.*

"Is later on today good?"

Damn.

"Uh, yeah. Just text me the address," I told her with a slight grimace. *Lord, why me?*

"Alright, see you then!"

Well then.

"Alright, um, bye."

I didn't wait for her to reply back before I ended the call. *I guess my past is resurfacing,* I thought, flopping back on my mattress.

***

"I'm sorry. You said what now?"

I rolled my eyes at Samantha's voice as we spoke on the phone about Haley's arrival. I did not have time for this.

"Girl, you heard me. She called me earlier this morning talking about she had some things to tell me. She said she wanted to meet sometime today."

"What did you say?"

"I told her sure."

I could tell she was shaking her head at me in disapproval. According to her, I was too nice. It was not my fault. I couldn't just say no. That would be rude. Plus, she is… or was my best friend. I still wasn't sure what to call her anymore, but I couldn't and wouldn't let a nigga come between a good friendship, no matter how much I loved him. It wasn't right.

"Girl, you so damn stupid! Why would you want to even be near that bitch after what you told me what she did? Shiiiiit, her ass would've gotten fought when it happened. Dite, you too fucking nice!"

Well then. I couldn't help that my daddy raised me this way. He always told me not to stoop to fighting unless it was necessary, because beauty didn't fight. She left that to the beast. I wasn't going to fight over anybody, and if that made me too nice or a punk, then so be it!

I exhaled. A part of me knew what Samantha said was true. I was too nice sometimes, especially when it came to Haley. She'd been my best friend since I was a child. It was hard to turn your back on shit like that. I couldn't just turn her away, not after all the shit we had been through. She'd always had my back. I remember when I used to be so insecure about my weight that I would always hide behind baggy clothing, although it was like ninety degrees outside. She came in and smacked some sense into me. She helped me lose a little weight where I was comfortable and made me see how beautiful I really was. I felt like I owed her so much because of it. Without her

51

help, I would probably feel like I had no purpose or that I was worthless.

Sighing I opened my mouth to speak, "Well shoot me then! I can't help it, and regardless of the situation, I still love and care for her." I snapped. I had already told her where Haley and I stood and why I was the way I was with her.

"What's love got to do with it?"

She sighed as if she were Tina Turner. I laughed at her childishness.

"But for real though, girl, you going to have to stop letting this girl off when you know how she is. I respect you, and I got your back. Let me get off your line though."

With that said, we said our goodbyes and hung up.

Ting

My notifications sound alerted me that I had a message. It was the same unknown number. Haley's number. I made a note to save this number for future purposes before I opened the text.

Haley: Let's me at Bartleby's around 3:45

Alright, I typed back. It was now 2:50 p.m., so I had enough time to get ready and be at the Cafe on time. After that, I tossed my phone on my bed and turned back

52

toward my closet as I stood dressed in my underwear. I had just hopped out of the shower not too long ago, and now I was looking for something to wear in order to meet Haley. I wasn't looking to impress her or anything, but sure enough, I wasn't going to let her see me just being casual. Yeah, I wanted to flex a little, but like I said, nothing too flashy.

After a few moments of pondering, I took out a pair of dark wash skinny jeans, an off the shoulder blue denim top, and a pair of white sandals, along with a black Givenchy bag. After getting dressed, I applied some gloss to my lips and perfume to my neck and chest before placing on my shades, pocketing my phone and keys, and heading out.

CHAPTER 5

<u>Aphrodite Samuels</u>

"My name is Tatiana, and I will be your waitress for this evening. Are you ready to order, or are you still looking?" greeted a waitress at the café. She was somewhat tall and curvy with a dark tan, green eyes, and blonde hair. A smile was on her face as she stared expectantly at me. I shook my head.

"No, but could you bring me some ice water and lemon? I'm waiting for a friend."

I grimaced as the word friend slipped out my mouth. *What do I even call her*? I sighed heavily. I really didn't know how to feel about seeing Haley again. I was already tripping because of Messiah, and now this?

"No problem! I'll get that back to you right away, ma'am," Tatiana spoke in an upbeat tone, bringing me out of my thoughts. I smiled and thanked her before she walked away. Sighing, I sat back and waited for my drink as well as Haley to arrive.

***

A few hours later

I could hear the narrator from SpongeBob state in my head as I slowly sipped on my lemon water. Right now, I was still waiting for Haley. It had been about fifteen minutes, but it felt like hours had passed since I'd arrived. If this girl didn't hurry her ass up, making me burn my gas to come all the way out here and still didn't show her face. I was going to give her five more minutes. If she didn't show in five, I'd be gone. She knows damn well I hate waiting for people especially if you said you were going to be here at a certain time. It's annoying and rude.

Bitch better have my money! Bitch better have my money!

This better be Haley, I thought, whipping out my phone and checking the caller I.D. *Damn, Omar,* I smacked my teeth and rolled my eyes before swiping the red tab to the left. *Ain't nobody got time for that man child's mess.* After declining his call, I was met by the face of my future husband, August Alsina. Messiah may have had my heart, but August was bae. I chuckled to myself and swiped my pattern password in before going through my contacts and scrolling for Haley's number that I had saved earlier this morning.

Where the fuck is that number? Did I even save it? I don't know, I thought I did.

"Oh, there she is. Aphrodite!"

I looked up at the person, widening my eyes in realization. This girl sure hadn't changed. Well, she did get thicker and a bit taller. She still had those same chocolate brown chinky eyes, along with her coffee brown hair that was currently in a wavy short cut style. Her light caramel skin seemed to glow as she smirked at me. Ugh! That damn face. Something was telling me she was up to no good. I shrugged. Haley was always the troublemaker. I plastered on a big Kool-Aid smile as I embraced her in a big hug, faking it until I believed it.

"Haley, omigod! Girl, how have you been?"

Lord, all this fakeness.

"You look so good," I gushed, pulling back a little to give her a once over.

She's cute or whatever but she ain't me.

"Oh, girl, you know how I do. But girl, look at you, looking all cute."

I could sense the fakeness in her voice and face, making me smirk on the inside. *Ooh, she's mad.*

"Thanks, girl. I've been hitting the gym and eating right." I laughed. She hummed in response. Gosh, the fakeness was real around here.

"Well good for you, girl. Anyway, let's get a move on. Shall we? Like I said, I have some things to tell you," she

56

boasted, sitting down on the other side of the table. We were currently sitting outside the restaurant under the lanterns attached to the pavilion. There weren't that many people here, although I thought it would be since this place was very popular.

"Okay, so the reason why I wanted see you was to tell you… I'm GETTING MARRIED!"

Who the hell?

"Oh, girl, those salads look good as fuck. I think I'm going to get the classic wedge salad. It comes with bacon, and you know I love me some bacon. What are you getting?" she asked, looking at me curiously, but if I wasn't mistaken, I could've sworn she was smirking evilly at me.

I shrugged it off and replied, "I'm in the mood for one of their chocolate rolls with a bit of pink lemonade."

Mmmm, I licked my lips at the thoughts of those sweet chocolate buns in my mouth. I inwardly laughed at the 'buns in my mouth' part of Jhene Aiko's song, *but you gotta eat the booty like groceries*. Eww! No thank you!

***

"So marriage… who's the lucky gu—"

Bitch better have my money! Bitch better have money! Oh my God! This man had truly lost his mind. My phone had been going off non-stop for the past thirty minutes, and I was 'bout ready to reach through this phone and strangle Omar's ol' dumb ass. What part of 'leave me the hell alone' did he not get? I gave a slight eye roll before clicking end on my phone and switching my notification volume to mute.

Haley's ass was being hella nosy, asking me who was calling me and why I didn't answer. I politely told her it was none of her business and kept it pushing. By the looks of it, she didn't like that. She held what seemed to be a permanent bitch mug on her face. I honestly paid it no mind. All I wanted to know was who this mystery man was who had the balls to try to turn a hoe into a housewife. Let me stop. Maybe she had changed. I mean, I hadn't seen or heard from her in like four years.

Bitch, now you know a tiger don't change its stripes! That girl will forever be a hoe. I gave a mental eye roll at my painfully blunt conscience before sighing.

"Sorry 'bout that. What were you saying?" I asked, giving her my full attention. A small smirk formed on Haley's face as she let out a sort of taunting laugh at my question and took a sip of her long island iced tea.

58

"Well, it happened about a month ago. I told him if he wasn't man enough to put a ring on it, then I would find another who would."

She chuckled, taking another sip of her drink. *If this heifer doesn't get to the point*!

"Let's not get into the details, but the *who* is someone you should know… Oh, there he is right there. Messiah, baby, over here!"

Ain't this 'bout a bitch?

CHAPTER 6

<u>Aphrodite Samuels</u>

I coughed.

"So y'all getting married? Oh, that's cool. Binky, I didn't know you and Jamie were related. Wow, small world."

Shut your ass up, Dite!

"I mean, that's straight or whatever."

Smooth, Dite… smooth. I could see the arrogant smirk form on Haley's face.

I wonder what would happen if I jump across this table and wrap my hands around her ne-nah let me stop. I ain't no criminal.

I inwardly groaned at my lack of sanity at the moment and rolled my eyes. I knew Haley just loved this. She was always the one for drama. She loved the fact that she could rile people up. Her ass was like a succubus when it came to this sort of thing. She fed off of it. It made her feel in control.

"Well, um… uh… it's good to see you, Bambie, again."

Damn, that voice. Just the sound of his deep velvety rich voice had my kitty purring in delight. Lord, I needed a new pair of underwear. *Lord Jesus give me the strength.*

60

"It's good to see you as well. Where did you go after the party?" I asked, trying to be as nonchalant as possible. At the mention of a party, Haley gave Messiah the side eye. Knowing Haley, she saw this as a problem. My guess was that he never told her he saw me, and by the looks of it, the worst case scenario was probably forming in her head. I mean, I did have him once. Why couldn't I again?

"Oh, so you went to a party without me? Mhm."

I laughed inwardly. Someone was feeling a bit insecure. I felt like Keyshia Cole right now. *I'll take your man! 'Cause I got it like that.* I inwardly laughed. Let me stop.

"It ain't even like that. It was a party for my lil' cousin. Bambie is his teacher," Siah replied, seeming frustrated at the situation. I mean, I would have been too. *Haley probably going to drill his ass when I leave. Sucks for him!*

"So why wasn't I invited to said party?"

Messiah smacked his teeth, shrugging Haley off. "It ain't even all that serious. It was just a party for lil' kids, so why you tripping?"

"You know what? Okay!"

61

Oh, she was mad. Man, I needed me some popcorn with the marshmallow sauce. Drama!

"Looks like y'all got some shit to settle. I'm going to just leave y'all be. Call me later!" I called over my shoulder as I put some distance between the three of us. The sooner I got away from him, the better. Just seeing this man in the flesh made me want to do some things, some very naughty things that I couldn't even put into words. *You need some vitamin D.* I shrugged. It wasn't a lie. I hadn't had any since my ex. I had to do better.

"Hey, wait. Will you be my maid of honor?"

I froze in place and slowly turned around. *No this heifer did not.* I wanted to decline, but it was like my mouth had a mind of its own.

"Yes."

Why did I say that?

CHAPTER 7

<u>Aphrodite Samuels.</u>

"Let me get this straight. Ol' bitch is getting married to the so-called love of your life, and you gonna be her maid of honor? Wow, you really are something, Aphro."

Samantha cackled at my predicament. *Some friend she is.* I rolled my eyes.

"It's not funny," I cried, flapping around in my bed. I was feeling like I did when I first saw him, thirsty. Fuck my life!

"I wanted to say no, but something made me say yes. Girl, I don't know!" I added. I don't know what the hell I was thinking when I agreed to that shit. Someone must've slipped something in my drink. Clearly, I wasn't thinking straight. Sammie wheeled around in my swivel desk chair around my room as she took in everything I told her. I couldn't be dealing with this shit, man! I thought I had left their asses in the past. Why must they pop back up in my life all of a sudden?

"Okay, baby girl. Sit up!" Sammie demanded, smacking my ass.

"You little ho—"

"Uh-uh. Get up, 'cause I'm gonna tell you what we're gonna do!" she spoke up, cutting me off. I sighed and

63

smacked my teeth. She was lucky I loved her. I rolled to my side before sitting up on my bed and stared at her. She sat in front of me, still in my swivel chair with determination in her almond hazel eyes.

"Look, baby girl. You need to stop letting this heifer win! So you best to dry those eyes 'cause girl, we're gonna get you all dolled up for this man tonight so that your ass can get some dick and stop acting like a mothafucking virgin!"

I gave out a throaty laugh and sighed in agreement. She was right. I couldn't let her win. I had to stop thinking about Messiah and just do me. He was about to get married. He didn't love me, nor had he ever, but wait.

"What man?"

"Oh! See, what had happened was, I told one of my colleagues he could take you out. His name is Derrick. He's an athletic trainer for Georgia State, and Lord, when I say the boy is fine, I mean godly."

She laughed sheepishly, making me frown. Was this hoe really trying to pimp me out? This bitch was crazy!

"So let me get this straight. You're basically my pimp? How much he pay you?" I asked sarcastically while rolling my eyes at her. The nerve of these heifers today!

64

"Girl, shut up! It ain't even all the serious." she spoke, smacking her teeth, ol' aggravating ass! I swear I was too nice.

"You know what? Just help me get dressed. When is he coming?"

Sammie nodded as she proceeded to help me pick out an outfit for tonight.

"He said 6:30."

I read the time on my phone. It read 4:45 p.m.

"Okay, so we ain't trying to be too flashy, but we have to show off those curves and those legs."

She rummaged through my closet before pulling out a burgundy bodycon mid-thigh dress.

"I know your ass gets cold quick, so I'm gon' let you wear that hooded gray cardigan you like so much over it. We're trying to keep it casual today."

I nodded my head before leaving her to finish picking out my outfit and heading to my bathroom so that I could wash. After a twenty-minute shower, I quickly dried off before moisturizing my body with some baby lotion. I then wrapped myself in a big baby blue fuzzy towel before stepping out of my bathroom. I walked back into my room to see that Sammie had left my outfit and undies laid out on the bed for me. I grabbed the pair of panties

65

she had picked out for me and smirked. *Black lace? Wow,
Samantha. Just wow.* She must have really thought I
would give ol' dude the booty tonight. *Well, it wouldn't
hurt.* I thought. Lord knows I needed it.

Shrugging, I quickly put on the panties as well as the
matching bra before slipping on my dress. I then slipped
on my white Arizona sandals that Samantha had paired
up with my outfit. After that, I added a bit of gloss to my
lips and mascara to my lashes before fixing my hair a bit.

"Let's take some pics for the gram," I told myself,
picking up my phone. I snapped a few pics in my full-
length mirror and uploaded them.

Knock! Knock!

A knock on the door alerted me that Derrick was here.
I grabbed my Michael Kors handbag and gray cardigan
from out of my closet then pocketed my keys and phone
before switching off the light to my room and leaving.

I made my way down the hall to my front door and let
out a low breath before opening it.

"Oh, you must be Derrick," I said, looking at ol' dude.
Lord Jesus, this man was blessed. He wasn't necessarily
tall, but he had a nice build on him. He had a nice little
short cut, neat beard, and mustache with some smoldering
dark brown eyes. He had the natural 'baby, let me lick

66

you up and down' look, and I swear my "parts" were screaming to be touched.

Fiendin' for the D. No shame! Lord. I took a breath and cleared my throat.

"I'm Aphrodite, but you can call me Dite."

He smiled a panty-dropper smile, making me blush. If he wasn't heaven sent...

"Aphrodite, as in the goddess of love, desire, and beauty? How beautiful."

He smirked, reaching out to caress my hands with his. I needed a cold shower. Sam hadn't prepared me for this!

"Uh, let's get going. Shall we?" I stuttered, quickly withdrawing my hand from his.

How about we just skip dinner and go straight to dessert?

No!

I scolded myself, but I couldn't lie. That wasn't a bad idea. I wouldn't mind if this man was deep inside of me. *Calm down, damn*! I sounded so parched.

Rolling my eyes, I pushed my inner hoe back into her corner and eyed Derrick. I watched him lick his bottom lip and smile before saying, "Alright, gorgeous. Let me show you to my car."

He took a hold of my hands once again and led me to his candy red coated 2014 Cadillac sedan. After a good little drive, we finally arrived at our destination. To say I was happy would be an understatement. *Lord Jesus, this man must've read mind.* I thought, staring longingly at the glass double doors.

"Oh snap! I know you ain't bring me to Blanco's! They have the best biscuits, man."

I grinned widely as I looked from my peripheral at Derrick as well as keeping a good eye on the restaurant. *Look at me, getting all excited about some food.* I laughed at myself. Blanco's was a sort of upscale, yet homey style restaurant on the upper east side of town. It was a Spanish themed restaurant where they served the best honey or cheesy herb biscuits and spicy crawfish linguine. Lord Jesus, please give me the strength. Derrick chuckled, making me blush. Even his laugh was sexy and had me feeling some type of way. I wasn't prepared for this!

"Samantha told me you love this place, and I aim to please in everything that I do."

Was it just me, or had I heard a sexual innuendo in that? Lord!

"I mean, it's cool. Whatever, boy! I'm hungry. Let's eat," I spoke coolly, hopping out of his car.

68

Messiah Lafayette

"Why you didn't tell me you saw Dite? I'm supposed to be your fiancée, but it's like you're always keeping secrets from me. Oh, but Bambie knows everything. Okay, I see."

I kissed my teeth and eyed Haley from my peripheral. The fuck? She was still on that shit. She ain't say nothing when we got home from meeting Dite or when a nigga was spending money on her ass all up and down this bitch, but now that a nigga was feeling comfortable and playing 2K, this broad wanted to talk. The fuck? What was she on?

"Man, don't even start that shit now. I already told you what it was from the jump."

I sighed tiredly, pausing the game. I was already done with the conversation, but if I knew Haley, I knew she wasn't finished until we started screaming back and forth at each other and then fucking like the world depended on it. That girl was a freak.

"Whatever, Messiah, or should I say Binky? You ain't telling me something, but it's okay. I'm gonna find out."

Bruh. I had to slide out this bitch before I got hit with that thirty. Her ass was on some other shit tonight. A nigga couldn't even enjoy himself.

69

Seeing Dite again had a nigga feeling some type of way. The way her body filled out her outfit made my mind flood with the images of her thick ass thighs spread apart, waiting for me to slide deep up I—— bruh, no!

Calm your ass down, Messiah! It ain't nothing but pussy.

I sighed slowly. "You know what, Hales? I ain't got time for this shit tonight. I know all you want to do is fuck, but sometimes a nigga gets tired of fucking."

Haley gasped in shock, making me roll my eyes. Ol' girl was 'bout dramatic. She gave me that 'nigga' look and mugged me.

"But you weren't too tired to fuck Dite."

The fuck?

"You really childish, bruh. I'll be back later."

With that being said, I pocketed my keys, slipped on my slides, and dipped.

***

Aphrodite Samuels

"Damn! Samantha ain't say shit about that appetite. Now I see why."

The fuck is he trying to say, I mused, clearing my throat and crossing my hands over my chest.

70

"What does that mean?"

I mean, I knew I had an appetite. Baby girl loved to eat, but sometimes, I still found myself getting defensive when it came to my appearance. I knew I was nowhere near ugly or as big as I used to be, but I still thought about that shit every once in a while.

Derrick laughed. The fuck was so funny? Shit, I wanted to laugh too.

"No disrespect, Goddess, but I mean, now I know why them thighs and that ass so thick. Don't get offended. I love me a girl who can eat," he said, throwing me a wink, causing blood to rush to my cheeks.

"Oh," I let out in a small voice, giggling uncontrollably. Why were people always saying that? I was nowhere near thick. I mean, sure, I had thighs and hips, but Coco, Chyna, and Nicki had me beat! Shaking my head, I rolled my eyes at Derrick. He still smiled that panty dropper smile at me as he watched me.

Creep.

Girl, now you know you love it!

And there she was again, that naughty, uncontrollable, ghetto, and violent little voice inside of my head!

Lord Jesus, give me the strength. .

"What's wrong, Goddess? Something on your mind?" Derrick spoke up, dragging me out of my thoughts. He stared at me questionably, rubbing small circles on my wrist. When had he gotten ahold of my hand? Coughing, I cleared my throat before speaking.

"Uh, I'm good. It's been stressful lately, but I'm good."

I smiled softly while swiftly pulling my hand from out of his. He laughed at my actions and nodded, going back to his food.

Messiah Lafayette

"Uh, I'm good. It's been stressful lately, but I'm good."

My eyes widened at the sound of her voice. I groaned, looking up at the sky. Really, G? Really? I sighed. All a nigga wanted to do was have a moment's peace as he sipped on a bit of liquor, but I couldn't even do that. Fuck my life, man. I shook my head at the turn of events and proceeded to scan the restaurant in search of my Bambie. I could hear her beautiful laugh bounce off the walls, making my chest tighten in longing. Why the fuck was she here?

Bruh, why you think she's here? Obviously not to see you!

As soon as that thought popped into my mind, my eyes zeroed in on them. She was smiling and being all shy with some nigga. I couldn't help but to be jealous. I see how it was. I knew it had been a while, but I thought she too would have been thinking about me like I'd thought about her. I couldn't really see ol' dude's face, because his back was turned to me. Her ass, sure enough, was cheesing real hard at whatever he was saying to her. I kissed my teeth. She had better not be trying to pass around my pussy. Lord knows I'd be going to jail.

But she ain't your girl, though.

73

Shrugging, I took another quick glance at Dite before turning back to the girl behind the counter.

"Give me about four tequila shots."

She nodded and got to work on my drinks.

"Rough day?" she asked, placing the four shots in front of me. *You don't even know the half.* I immediately downed the shots and winced at the burning sensation I felt at the base of my neck. *Let me get my ass up out of here,* I thought before hopping up. I took out a few bills and gave it to her.

"Keep the change." I said. I low key stared at their asses as I slid past them. I clenched my fist. All my thoughts ran through my mind when I thought of this nigga taking her home. *She might let him hit. Her ass better not try me on some lame shit. That pussy is mine.* It pissed me off that I couldn't do anything about it, because she wasn't my girl. Man, I should've stayed my ass home.

***

Aphrodite Samuels

"So you gonna let me get your number?"

Derrick popped his mouth as he did a little dougie movement before continuing.

"Or nah?"

74

I rolled my eyes and laughed. He must have been feeling himself.

"Boy, you already fed me and told me I'm pretty, so you're dismissed!" I playfully snapped, giving him the 'swerve' hand. He hummed and tapped his chin. We were standing in front of the door to my apartment just cheesing at one another. That little hoe inside me wanted his Twix, but I refrained. I didn't want to give it up on the first night. I wanted to see how far this would go. I hopped my ass on into bed with Messiah like it was nothing, and look how that had turned out. I mean sure, Siah and I were never together, but that shit didn't matter. I always thought we had something, but I guess that's what I got for thinking.

"Oh, so it's like that? I thought we had something special, Aphrodite! I was ready to buy a ring for your finger and Jimmy's for your feet. Girl, I was about to make you say my name, say my name, when I'm deep insid—"

I quickly placed my palm over his mouth and looked around to see if anybody was outside on my floor. Mrs. Kathy was always in someone's business around here. If she were to hear this, no telling what she would be thinking or doing.

75

"Boy, don't play!" I snapped at him in a whisper.

"You're something serious, man."

He simply smiled and kissed my right hand which covered his mouth. I kissed my teeth and withdrew my hand. *He thinks he's cute.*

"So, you going to give me them digits, or do I need to persuade you?"

He flexed cockily, making me roll my eyes.

"I mean, I'll even take your Kik as a starter."

I needed a glass of Nay after this.

"Knowing Samantha, she probably already gave you my number."

I gave him a look, noticing his eyes spark up at my accusation. *That bitch.*

"Y'all are something else."

I shook my head and walked into my home before shutting the door in his face.

"I'm gonna call you, and you better pick up, Goddess!" he called from the other side. Lord! Now I really needed a cold shower.

Messiah Lafayette

"What took you so long?"

I damn near jumped out of my skin when Haley's ass popped up on some creep shit as soon as I opened the door. Her ass was about to get popped fucking around. Good thing God was looking out for me and her.

"Just getting something to drink," I replied and sat on the couch to watch TV as she followed me from the door to the couch.

"Met anybody?"

I said no. Just hearing her asking felt as though I had been set up. Did she know that Dite would be at Blanco's? I doubted it. Haley and Dite were close, but it had been a good little minute since they'd seen each other. I didn't even think they were all that close anymore anyway.

"I'm gonna take a shower," I said. I got up and headed to the bathroom. I bet Haley's ass was gon' try me with that mess again. I could tell by the way her left eye twitched that she wanted some answers. For what? I didn't know, and I didn't give a fuck. I didn't have time for that shit. A nigga was tired and angry. All I wanted was some peace for once.

CHAPTER 8

Aphrodite Samuels

"You disgust me!"

The fudge is she on about now?

"Please, my lovely best friend. Do tell me what I did now." I said sarcastically, rolling my eyes at Sam. For some reason, ever since she so-called invited herself over, all she had been doing was mean mugging me, and quite frankly, it was getting annoying. *I do not have time for this.* I thought, mentally rolling my eyes. I was supposed to be at church right now, but no. My dumb ass chose to stay home and "relax". Samantha's ol' bipolar self, wasn't having that, and although she seemed to be highly upset with me, that sure enough hadn't stopped her from eating up all my Lean Cuisine hot pockets. The nerve of people these days! I shook my head and gave her the 'go on' look. This girl was too dramatic for her own good. I didn't know how or why I put up with her. I guess I was attracted to the crazies.

"Bitch. I ain't crazy. My mama got me checked. Fawk you mean?"

Wait, what?

"You're talking out loud, bitch. Damn! Just so you know, you ain't shit without me!"

78

For the love of everything that was good. I inhaled a deep breath and slowly let it out and looked at her ass. I stared at her from across the room, left eye twitching a bit. The things I would like to do right now. I was going to end up on snapped because of her ass. I swear.

"Samantha, I do not have time for this. Can you please tell me how the fuck I disgust you? I didn't even d—"

"See, that's your problem now! You ain't do shit!" she exclaimed, cutting me off, causing me to throw her a mean mug of my own. Lord Jesus, please give me the strength not to take my hands and strangle this girl. She was just asking for me to wring her neck.

"What—"

"All I asked was for you to do one thing, yet you couldn't even manage to do that. God, do you know nothing?"

The fuck was she talking about?

"You couldn't just have stepped out of character this one time?" she asked, cutting my question off. Maybe she needed a slice of cake, a little sugar in her system. All this hostility on a Sunday? Lord, help me!

"Look, Samantha! I'm going to need you to calm down just a little."

I pinched my index finger and thumb together, gesturing how far she needed to lower her attitude.

"It is 9:00 on a Sunday. What could have made you this mad that got you pulling a Hulk in my living room?"

"You just don't get it, DITE! You had it. You fucking had it, and you know what you do with it? You tossed it to the side. All my hard work wasted!"

What? I scratched my head in confusion and starred in her ablaze eyes.

"What I did? Huh? What I do?" I asked childishly, feeling a bit unnerved by the way she looked at me. This heifer was legit crazy.

"You didn't do shit! I practically gave him the map and key to get to that old dusty treasure chest you keep hidden, and what do you do? I'm going to tell you what you did, change the mothafucking locks! I tried to get you some good hot and much needed dick, and this is how you repay me? Sending that man home cold, hungry, and alone. How dare yo——"

Okay, I'd heard enough. This girl had officially lost her God-given mind.

"Girl, you're mad because I ain't a hoe? Excuse me for having class, unlike you, your royal thotness!" I remarked sarcastically, sucking my teeth. I needed a drink. Sighing,

80

I rolled my eyes and turned away from Samantha to get an ice-cold bottle of nay out of my fridge.

"You want some?" I asked, grabbing two wine glasses before cracking open the bottle.

"I mean, shit. I don't like you right now, but I can drink."

I nodded and filled up her cup and mine. She graciously took her glass as I did the same.

"Now continue. Are you mad because I'm not a hoe or…?"

She let out a frustrated huff before taking a sip of her wine.

"See, this is where you fucked up. I gave you a heavenly sculpted, delicious looking, sexy ass man who you COULD have ravished and molded into your own, yet you wanted to be Miss Bougie, with your uptight ass!"

Whatever. I sighed and rolled my eyes. Lord have mercy on my soul. Why did I surround myself with crazy people?

"Okay, Sam. You got it. I'm going to go back to my room, though. Make like Calvin, and be breezy!"

***

81

"Are you still mad?" I asked Sam who, by the way, decided she was going to make herself at home in my living room whilst I slept. I swear, this girl was lucky I loved her. Her greedy ass had not one, not two, but three boxes of Domino's pizza and a side of wings just casually sitting in front of her on the table that sat between the TV and the sofa she was occupying. How rude! I bet her ass wasn't going to save me anything. Samantha shrugged at my question as she nibbled on a chicken bone. That bitch swears she was doing something. There wasn't an ounce of meat on that bitch. She was gon' fuck around and be missing a pinky or two, ol' fat ass.

"Samantha, you know damn well ain't nothing left on that bone, so why your ass over there trying hard as shit to get something that ain't there? You think it's going to be better because you drench it in some ranch? I can't."

Sam sucked her teeth and gave me the one finger salute as if saying *bitch, please*. All I could do was laugh. That bitch was a character.

Once my laughter died down, my mind went back to last night. I knew for a fact I wasn't on that booty call life, but it wouldn't hurt to be more open at times. However, that openness that I had when I first met Messiah was what led up to me having a broken heart and confused

82

feelings on love. I understood that Messiah and Derrick were two different people, but that doubt was still there. I knew for a fact my heart couldn't take another heartbreak like that. That shit was life altering. The feeling of giving your all to someone and having them turn around and smash and stomp your heart into the ground was painful.

Knowing that you were never good for that person can make you feel some type of way. You try to change yourself in hopes to gain their attention, although they're already in another relationship. You crave their affection, even though you know you won't get it. It's hard. If it wasn't for my dad, I couldn't have made it this far. He was there when I would cry constantly to him about seeing Messiah with Haley, staying up late just to make sure I was alright and telling me that I couldn't let Messiah define me. He knew how I felt. He went through the same shit with my mom, but he survived. We survived. I didn't need Messiah. All I could say was that I wished Messiah and Haley the best. I couldn't be petty. Shit, he had chosen who he wanted.

I shook my head, coming back to reality just in time to hear Sam ask," what are we about to get into today, best friend?"

I sucked my teeth. These hoes these days always wanted to catch an attitude, but then they wanted you to spend time with 'em. I wasn't trying to do shit with her ass. Knowing her, we were just going to hang out with a few of her carrot eating friends at Planet Fitness or some shit. Although she ate like she had four stomachs, she was a personal trainer. *Ain't that some shit?*

I gave her that look and rolled my eyes.

"Bitch, I am not hanging out with you today. I know all you do on Sunday is hang out with them leaf eating mothafuckers and head to the gym. Ol' girl talking 'bout 'let's go. Aphrodite! You can do it! I believe in you!' The last time I was with you, bitch, all I was doing was walking on a treadmill. The fuck you got to believe in me for?"

Sam laughed one of those infectious but annoying cackle-like laughs while trying to nod her head in agreement to where I was coming from with my reply. She knew her friends did the most. They all ate, lived, and breathed fitness. Samantha, on the other hand, was in the middle. She liked to stay in shape, but don't you dare try to come between her and her mama's honey butter biscuits. You would die if you dared.

84

"I mean, they're not all that bad. Melissa likes you,"
she said. I shrugged.

"Nah, I'm good."

CHAPTER 9

Aphrodite Samuels

I need a one dance

Got a Hennessy in my hand

One more time 'fore I go

Higher powers taking a hold on me

I need a one da—

Drake's' voice rang from my purse as I browsed through a blouse rack. *Who could that be?* I rolled my eyes in annoyance. It seemed that every time your girl wanted to go shopping, somebody always wanted to call me and ask for something. Rolling my eyes once more, I fished my phone out of my bag and swiped the green tab to the right.

"Aphrodite Samuels speaking. How may I help you?"

"Damn, Bambie. You still answer the phone like that?"

Bruh, say it ain't so.

"What? You can't speak no more?"

I said nothing. All I could do was think, *how the fuck did he get my number*? I turned my eyes up toward the sky and shook my head. *Lord, you're testing me.* All I wanted to do was do some simple shopping at Macy's, but

86

I couldn't even do that. First, Samantha's ass wanted to throw her hissy fit earlier, and now this shit. What was going on here?

"Hello? I know you're there. I hear you breathing. I missed you, best friend."

I could've sworn there was an ounce of sincerity in his voice, but then again, I could've still been just hearing shit. We were never just best friends. I sighed. *Let it go, Dite.* I told myself. And with that in mind, I replied.

"How are you? Does Haley need any help with the wedding or something?"

"Nah, she good. I'm good. What about you?"

The nerve...

Messiah Lafayette

"I'm fine. Nothing new, but if you didn't want anything in particular, let me call you back or something," Bambie spoke before hanging up. *Fuck.*

"Who was that?"

I sucked my teeth and mugged Haley as her ass latched herself onto my arm. We were so-called shopping for our wedding, but she and that rat ass friend of hers, Mariah, didn't seem to need me. *She better gon' somewhere with that shit, always trying to sneak up on a nigga like that.*

"Don't worry about it. What's in those bags?" I asked, nodding toward the bags in her hands. It was probably some useless ass shit. Her ass loved spending my money, but I loved her. Now see, Bambie wouldn't do shit like this. She was the type that would make her own money and pay for her own shit. She was Miss Independent. Damn, I missed her ass. She wasn't trying to hear a nigga before. She was probably with ol' dude from the bar. Just thinking about last night had me vexed. The way she was smiling at his ass had me feeling some type of way. I should've been the only one she smiled like that at. Fuck! Why did things have to be so fucked up?

"Messiahhhhhhhhhhhhhhhhhhhhhhhhh."

88

My soul damn near left my body at the sound of Haley's whiny ass voice. She needed to stop before I forgot who she was. She was always catching a nigga off guard with that shit. *The fuck she want now?*

"What, man? Damn."

Both she and Mariah gave me a stank look and rolled their eyes. I didn't even know why Mariah's ass had an attitude. I wasn't fucking her. She'd better take that pissy ass attitude on somewhere, before I set that shit straight. I ain't have time for her or Haley's ass right now.

Haley let out a little annoyed huff, placing her hands on her hips with that same stank ass mug on. Between her and Bambie's ass, I was about three seconds away from catching a case.

"You know what? Never mind, since you want to have an attitude. Let's go, Mariah!"

Aphrodite Samuels

"Guess what? He called me."

"Derrick?"

"No. Messiah."

"Bitch, you lying. What did he say?"

I then went on to tell Samantha about my brief chat with Messiah while at Macy's. Right now, I was in my apartment just chilling and watching Netflix while on the phone with Samantha. I had to catch up on *Heroes*. Plus, all I felt like doing was curling up into a ball, eating, and binge-watching shit. It seemed like Messiah was always able to put me in this mood. It was like after I spoke to him or saw him now, I just felt the need to stop everything I was doing and think about old shit, even though I knew I shouldn't. The more I thought about our old memories, the more I felt like I was falling apart. I couldn't allow that. *Damn, when did my life get so fucked up?*

Samantha's laughter brought me out of my thoughts, making me suck my teeth in annoyance. I felt like Kevin Hart right now. Just laugh at my pain.

"Your life, Dite. I can't."

She laughed obnoxiously with a little snort at the end, all up in my ear with that shit. I kissed my teeth and shook my head at the nerve of her ol' obnoxious ass.

"Man, Dite. I love you. Your life right now is hilarious! I love it."

"I did not call you just so you can laugh at my expense. You are supposed to be supportive. Why are you still laughing?" I asked, annoyed as she continued to cackle on the other side. I swear I hated her. She huffed and heaved, trying to contain herself, talking about some *I can't breathe.* Ugh. It wasn't even that serious, man.

"Are you done?" I asked impatiently after what seemed like forever. This girl did the most.

"Nah, for real though, Dite. Your life is a mess and sounds like ol' dude wants him some SUGAR from Miss Aphrodite Samuels. But we don't want that, do we? We want us some Derrick, right?" she responded after catching her breath, causing me to pause. *Wasn't Derrick supposed to call me? What happened to that? You know what, let's not even get into all that. I'm good.*

"Dite, girl, are you listening?" Sam asked, bringing me back to reality. I really needed to stay out of my head. *Wait, what? Does that even make sense? Fuck it. It's whatever.*

91

"DITE!"

I shrieked a little at the sound of my name being screamed into my right ear.

"My bad, Sam. Yeah, I'm listening. And to answer your question, I don't know what I want. My heart is yearning for Messiah. The more I try to fight it, the more I run toward it. He was my first. It's hard to get over that, and the shit he did to me really hurt me. I can't forget that, even though it was so long ago."

I paused, realizing how true that actually was. Messiah was and maybe still is my heart. I didn't want him to be, but that's how it was. He had impacted my life in a way I couldn't explain. And then there was Derrick. I didn't really know much about him, but I felt like I wanted to. It was complicated.

"I hear what you saying, Dite, and I get it. He was your first love and your first, but you have to realize you can't keep going on like this. He obviously doesn't care about your feelings, or he wouldn't be marrying your so-called best friend, a bitch that was like your sister. Just so you know, she ain't your sister. I am your sister, and I'm going to have your back regardless of how you choose to live your life. Follow your heart, baby girl, but remember that what you want isn't always what you need."

92

***

What you want isn't always what you need.

I allowed Samantha's words from earlier to wash over me for a good little minute as if trying to wrap my head around what she was trying to convey to me. It wasn't really all that easy to understand as it sounded. I had to take in the fact that my heart wanted Messiah, but my heart also felt used and bruised by him as well. My heart seemed to be just as confused as my mind. It's either I missed him or fuck him. I could do bad all by myself, or with him was where I wanted to be. I was stuck between a rock and a hard place. Should I build a bridge and get over it, or should I stay and ponder on what could've been? The answer seemed to be easy, but Lord knows it wasn't.

I sighed. Why did shit have to get so fucked up? *Why you had to go and do this to us*, my mind silently asked Messiah. What was I supposed to do? Samantha was right. Messiah wasn't what I needed, but it sure enough felt like it. *God, I think I'm going crazy. I need a nap.* I thought. My brain was officially tired of all this thinking. And on top of that, I had to work in the morning. I couldn't have all this stress on my mind and then have to deal with twenty little ones the next day. Nah, that wasn't

93

going to fly for me. You know what? Let me stop thinking about this shit and take my ass to sleep.

CHAPTER 10

Aphrodite Samuels

"Come to the carpet. Come and join me at the carpet, children," I sang, clapping lightly and ushering my kids to the round carpet that laid under the alphabet wall next to our class library. Once everyone was seated, I stopped my singing and took a seat along with them.

"Okay, little ones. Catch a bubble."

I watched as everyone shut their mouths abruptly while also placing their hands on their folded laps. I smiled. Why couldn't everything be this easy?

"Now that everyone's quiet, I'm going to tell you what it is that we are going to do today. Can anybody guess?" I asked, holding up a packet of bean plant seeds. We were going to be planting today as our main activity for the day after reading *Oh Say Can You Seed* by Dr. Seuss. It was a part of our all about nature theme for the week.

"Yes, Emma. What do you think we are going to do today?" I asked the small redhead who had her hand raised slightly. She kind of reminded me of Merida in appearance. She had a head full of fiery red locks and a small fragile figure to pair with it. She was such a bright little girl for her age, but she was also very shy and soft-spoken.

95

"We're going to be planting today?" she answered softly, blushing slightly with her head held down. I nodded in response before continuing my instructions.

"Exactly! We are going to be planting bean plants, and after they grow to a certain point, you guys can take them home. But before we do that, we have to know a few things about plants. Dr. Seuss is going to tell us the things we need to know in this book, *Oh Say Can You Seed*."

I paused and held up the book for everyone to see before continuing.

"Now, let's hear what Mr. Seuss has to say about plants."

With that being said, I started the story.

**

Messiah Lafayette

"Nigga, why are you still over here?" Trey, my best man and nigga since day one, asked. I ain't feel like staying home, so I came over. Haley's ass and that damn Mariah were talking loudly on the phone all damn morning, talking shit as usual, and I ain't have time.

"Really, Trey? I thought we were better than this." I spoke sarcastically. His ass was already trying to get rid

96

of me. It wasn't anything but 5:00. Shit, what was another hour?

Trey gave me that 'nigga' look, causing me to sigh. I knew I was in the wrong. I was over here bugging the shit out of him just with my presence, but what the fuck was I supposed to do? I couldn't go home, and a motherfucker had problems on top of problems, man.

I smacked my teeth. I need to get out my feelings.

"Sy, my nigga, you good ? A nigga over there spacing out and shit."

Shit, I had forgotten he was here. I needed to stay from out of my head. That probably didn't make any sense, but fuck it.

"Man, I been stressing. Haley's ass, this wedding, and Bambi—"

"Wait a fucking minute? Are you talking about full lip, thick thighs, and hips Aphrodite AKA Bambie? The one who had your nose wide open in college? She back? Oh shit. She is cool with Haley. Damn, Sy. You stuck."

I mugged Trey from my peripheral. This nigga just had to say some shit like that, up there and gon' pause the whole entire game, just to say that. Talking about full lip, thick thighs, and hips, forever trying my shit. He knew I didn't play that shit about Bambie. That was mine. She just didn't understand.

"Bruh, the fuck did you say? Don't get you shit split, my nigga."

To that, he held up his hands in defense and shook his head before unpausing the game. His ass was over there playing FIFA while my ass sitting in my feelings like a female.

"My bad, Sy, but I'm just being honest. Bambie was bad. Ain't no telling how good she looks now, but what about ol' girl?"

Shit, he ain't have to ask me twice.

"Bruh, she got my head all types of fucked up! Bambie's glow up is real. Baby filled out nicely, but the thing is, she a bit too thick. All that ass ain't just pop out of nowhere. She's been fucking. That shit doesn't sit right with me, but I can't be feeling this way, right? I'm getting married, and she ain't my girl."

I paused and thought about that last part. *She ain't my girl.* Why the fuck was I getting so worked up about her ass? I mean, we weren't together and never were. She was just my best friend.

Nah, nigga. Don't start that best friend shit. You know y'all were more than friends.

98

True, but that's my baby, or at least she was. She just wanted something different. I had to respect that, right? Damn! Sighing, I ran my hands over my face and shook my head. I was feeling like a Drake ass nigga. I could write a song with all this shit I was holding in. Trey sat silently, seeming well invested into the game, but I knew he was listening. After a good little minute, he spoke up.

"Well you said it yourself. She ain't your girl, but we all know y'all both felt some type of way for each other back in the day. Haley clouded your judgment, bruh. I thought you and Bam were end game. You chose to wife Haley and didn't expect that shit between you and Bambie to fade. In the end, this is your life, Sy. Do you? Figure out what or who you want before it's too late."

Aphrodite Samuels

What am I going to eat today? I asked myself as soon as I unlocked the door to my apartment. *I could go for a burger, but ain't nobody got time for that. Shit, Ramen it is, I guess.* Good thing I had some sour cream and hot sauce. You couldn't just eat plain Ramen. Nah, you had to finesse it. I grabbed a packet of chicken flavored Ramen, popped it into a pot, along with some water, and let it cook. After they were cooked, I added the hot sauce and sour cream in a bowl along with my noodles and grabbed a water. I took my food and drink back to the sofa and sat down to eat while I watched *Catfish* reruns.

I was just about to go to work on these noodles when Ri Ri's voice blared from the kitchen, causing me to suck my teeth in annoyance. I had left my phone in the kitchen along with my bag, and I did not feel like getting up. My feet were hurting, and I was tired and hungry. I really wasn't in the mood to be messed with right now. Kindergarten was no joke. Those kids were savages on the playground! You couldn't stay seated. You were always moving around, making sure everybody was okay. At least that's what you do when you're invested in what you're doing. I'd see some of the other teachers during recess, and all those bitches did was gossip instead of

100

looking out for the kids. I hated that shit! Why teach if you were not going to give 100%? It wasn't fair to the kids if you acted like they were just another paycheck to you, but I was going to be Kermit, so that was none of my business, for now, at least.

Bitch better have my money! Bitch better have my money! Bitch better have my, bitch better have my—.

These motherfuckers! Ugh! I might as well get up. They were lucky I'm nice. I heaved a heavy sigh before hopping up from my seat. I was going to have to change my number. Bitches always wanted to call me when I was trying to do me. I grabbed my phone off the counter and checked the caller ID which caused me to suck my teeth. *That damn Haley. The fuck she want now*? Rolling my eyes, I coughed a little to clear my throat before answering.

"Yeah," I voiced, not really feeling like being boujie at the moment. "My bad, girl. I mean what's up? Do you need anything? Messiah said y'all are straight."

I could just see the gears in her head turning as she took in what I said, and if I knew anything about Haley, I knew that she was very "protective" if you will of what was hers. Something told me she didn't know anything about our chat, but that was none of my business. I just wanted to get back to my noodles and show.

"Mmm, so you and Messiah talked? Okay, when was this?" she asked bluntly. I could hear the anger in her voice. That bitch was mad, and I didn't know why. It ain't like we fucked.

"Yesterday, but what's up though?" I asked again, completely ending any continuation of the whole Messiah ordeal. That was their business, and she did what the fuck she wanted. She better leave me out of it.

"Mmm, but look, girl. Since you are my maid of honor, I want you to meet my bridesmaids. We're going to be discussing some things for my wedding tomorrow."

The fuck did she say it like that for? What was she trying to say? You know what? I was going to cool it. It wasn't even worth contemplating.

"Okay, but what time? I have to stay at work until 4:30." I told her. Man, I wanted to hang up right now. My noodles were probably going to be cold. Haley's ass acted like she didn't know what I did for a living. I worked every day of the week, talking about tomorrow. This heifer!

Haley sucked her teeth a little, and I could tell she was rolling her eyes at me. *Bitch, is you mad because I*

got shit to do? Like, I don't have a man to take care of me
and pay the bills.

"Fine, Dite. We can do it on Saturday."

This girl and her attitude! The shit was on ten, and I
was on E. I didn't have time. *Let me just end this shit.*

"That sounds good, but I gotta go. Bye!"

With that being said, I hung up on her ass and went
back to my food. I stuffed my face with noodles and
sighed happily. It was just me and my food as it should
have been from the jump. It was simply blissful.

Messiah Lafayette

I sat in deep thought, trying to come to an understanding of the words Trey had said earlier. The shit seemed so foreign to me. *Figure out what or who you want before it's too late.* What the fuck did I want? Man, Bambie used to be my heart. No labels, but she was my girl. And Haley, Haley was cool when she wanted to be. She was there for me when Bambie broke my heart. Why the fuck did she have to lead a brotha on?

Look at you, ol' Drake ass nigga.

Bru——

"Really, Messiah? Really?"

Man, this woman here, always sneaking up on me and shit. I was going to pop her ass in the mouth if she wasn't careful. I was already spazzing out and shit. The fuck was she on about now? All a nigga wanted to do was sit and think in peace, but nah. This woman wanted to creep her ass into the kitchen on some dumb shit. I gave her a look and shook my head. I wasn't even going to say anything.

"So you going to act like you don't know what I'm talking about?"

Man, I ain't even say shit. I sucked my teeth and coughed. I was just gon' wait this one out. I was gon' let

104

her speak her mind. I ain't have time for her shit right now.

"So you don't have shit to say? Okay, tell me why Dite talking about y'all had talked yesterday. Was she who you were talking to yesterday? Don't lie to me, Messiah. You think I'm stupid."

Man...

"You called her? Why are you calling her? How you even get her number? So you're sneaking behind my back now, Messiah?"

I shook my head, taking in everything she was saying and made a hand gesture for her to continue. I wasn't gon' stop her.

"I know y'all had a little thing back in the day, but please don't try me. You're my man, and she's my best friend. That shit doesn't and better not mix!"

With that being the last thing she said, she made a sharp turn and left the room. I laughed. This bitch was about crazy. It wasn't even like me and Dite had a whole conversation. Shit had ended as quickly as it had begun. Dite ain't want shit to do with a nigga. Haley had better pipe that shit down. I mean, didn't I always come home to her? The fuck she thought I was creeping for? That wasn't me. I was raised better. You know what, I ain't even got

105

the energy to deal with this right now. I'm just going to forget all this bullshit for now and ignore Haley's aggravating ass as much as I can.

CHAPTER 11

<u>Aphrodite Samuels</u>

It had been approximately two days since my call
with Haley, since Wednesday to be exact. Haley's ass
hadn't called me since, and quite frankly, I was glad. I
hadn't really played a big part in the wedding, but I was
already over it. I was just ready for Haley and her man to
leave my life again. Maybe then I could finally get some
peace and do me for a change. Right now, I was currently
watering our class plants while my kids were at lunch.
Today had been a fairly good day thus far. The kids were
great, and I had managed to get a lot of their work graded.
All I had left was to separate their work into their student
folders. I'd do that later.

I need a one dance.

Bruh, I could've sworn I left that phone on silent.
Who could it be now? I grabbed my phone from off my
desk and looked at the caller ID. It read unknown. *Wait,
should I answer this? What if it's some creep? But then
again, Avery probably gave my number out again, like he
did with Haley. Ugh! Let me gon' ahead and answer this
call.*

"Aphrodite Samuels speaking. How may I help you?"
I asked. I hoped this wasn't another work of my daddy,

107

giving my number out to people without my permission and shit. He did me wrong with that Haley one.

"Yo, Goddess. Are you there?"

Really, dude? Really? After all this time. Bruh was really bugging. Lord Jesus, give me the strength. He was really playing himself right now. *I can't. You know what? Let me calm down.* I was getting way too worked up about this, and I had only fifteen minutes left in my lunch period. *Dite, calm down.* I breathed in a little, calming myself down.

"Hey, Derrick."

"That's more like it. How's my goddess?"

The nerve!

"I'm good and yourself?" I asked with a roll of the eyes. He really tried it. I was not going to jump to conclusions, though. I just didn't like when men put up fronts. If you're not interested or have someone else in the picture, let me know. Don't waste my time.

"I'm straight. Been trying to open up my own athletic center. Had to go and take a few business courses so I can get my shit together."

So that's why he hadn't hit me up earlier.

And here your ass go assuming the worst and shit.

108

I mentally rolled my eyes at myself. Well, good thing was he didn't have baby mama drama. Lord knows I wasn't trying to get into that again. I mean, Omar's ex wasn't crazy or anything. I ain't even know her like that, but that back and forth shit with Omar over his past life was something I wasn't trying to get into with someone else.

"Goddess?"

"Sorry, umm, that's good to hear. You're trying to be a businessman and things. I feel you. That's very admirable," I spoke genuinely. It was refreshing to see a man who had goals and ambitions such as this. Men who want to better themselves in life through hard work, education, and dedication were hard to find these days. This day and age, people were consumed by social media and material things. They didn't recognize that you have to put in work to do great things.

Derrick laughed.

"I'm glad you think so. You probably thought a nigga was on some of that lame shit, saying I'm gon' text you and then don't, but that ain't my style. I hope you weren't mad, though," he responded. *Well shit, if he ain't just read my previous thoughts.*

"I mean, just a little, but I respect your honesty. And listen, I'm at work now, so I'll talk to you later?"

After one last reply from him, we said our goodbyes and hung up. *Let me get back to work before I get caught up in my feelings again.*

***

"Why are you always here?"

This bitch had made herself at home in my house yet again. I really needed to take that key away from her and see if I could get my locks changed. She was getting too comfortable and eating up all my food.

"Firstly, why haven't you been grocery shopping? I needs my pizza rolls! Secondly, calm that ass down! You know you enjoy my company."

I rolled my eyes at her nonchalant attitude and mean mugged the fuck out of her ass as I watched her flip from channel to channel. This hoe had really taken the 'mi casa es su casa' to a whole other level. This made me glad I'd never had a sibling growing up. My space was my space, but now that shit wasn't gon' fly. I had a sister from another mister named Samantha now. She was lucky I wasn't a violent person.

"Bitch, why are you always spacing out on me? Pay attention!" Samantha snapped, bringing me back to reality. *Heifers these days*!

"Whatever, Sam. Stop eating up all my food, and I won't have to go grocery shopping all the damn time!" I replied back, slipping off my Adidas and dropping my bag in the seat next to her.

"Go on GrubHub, and order some food. I'll go shopping sometime this weekend or something."

With that being said, I went and changed into some leggings and a T-shirt before coming back to the living room.

"Mexican good for you?"

I nodded, plopping down on the left side of the sofa. My eyes lit up as soon as they registered what she was watching.

"Caillou!"

Yes, bitch. *Caillou* was my shit. Samantha and I loved ourselves some PBS Kids and Sprout. It hadn't changed much since my childhood, unlike Disney Channel and Cartoon Network. All the classics still came on. If not, you could find it on demand. I didn't' give a fuck what anybody said. You were never too old for *Caillou*, *SpongeBob*, or *Wow Wow Wubbzy*.

111

"Yass, bitch! You know *Caillou* get me turnt,"
Samantha said, matching my excitement. I swear our
asses became kids when it came to PBS Kids. We were so
childish, but it worked. That's why we worked. The rest
of the evening was spent watching shit on Sprout, eating
Mexican food, and just vibing.

CHAPTER 12

Aphrodite Samuels

My guard immediately went up as soon as I approached the restaurant Haley had told me to come to today. It was Saturday. Apparently. I had to meet her so-called friends for her wedding. I didn't know anything about these women, and I didn't want to, but for Haley's benefit. I had to. Like I said, I was already over this wedding. but me being a good person. I wasn't going to ruin her day by being a bitch. That ain't in me.

I immediately spotted Haley's slender figure dressed in a long. flowy ivory summer dress. just sitting there trying to look cute.

Over there kee-hee-heeing and shit. Let me stop talking, well, thinking shit. She was all smiles and shit until her eyes landed on me. Her once genuine smile became fake as ever. causing me to inwardly roll my eyes. That child always has an attitude.

"Hey, Dite!" she yelled. waving me over with a too wide to be real Cheshire cat grin on her face. God, when did my best friend become so fake? We really have been out of each other's lives for far too long. I barely recognize her sometimes. but that wasn't gon' stop me from being cordial while she was here. I mean, I could be petty, but I was gon' keep my cool.

"Let me introduce you to the rest of the girls," she chirped as soon as I approached the table.

"I would like you to meet my bridesmaids; Mariah, Niamey, and Asia." Haley said, introducing me to her friends.

Mariah was your stereotypical white girl; blonde hair, blue eyes, and skinny. Niamey seemed to be very curvy, with ice gray eyes and olive toned skinned. Asia favored Keke Palmer but not in a sense that they could be twins. I was no hater. They were all beautiful and seemed cool enough. I just hoped they weren't anything like Haley. One of those is enough for me, or hell, for anyone.

"Hey, I'm Aphrodite. Most people call me Dite, and I am the maid of honor as well as this girl's…" I paused and gestured toward Haley before continuing.

"Best friend." I added, inwardly rolling my eyes as Mariah mugged me. This bitch was already on a bad start. I wasn't a violent person, but she better not test me. I didn't even know ol' girl, but she already had an attitude.

"You're Haley's best friend, but you slept with her husband? Oh okay."

114

I stale face this broad. What the fuck was she on? For one, I didn't know the hoe. Secondly, I had him first, but I let his ass go when he got with Haley. She was over there talking like I was some kind of home-wrecker. She had better slow her roll. *If you gon' come at me, then always come correct. The nerve of this hoe. They ain't even married, yet you're talking about "husband". Girl, bye!*

"I'm going to be Ray J right now. So it is true that I hit it first, but that's not why we're here, is it? This is Haley's day, so don't get it twisted. What happened between Messiah and me ain't nobody's business but ours. So, boo boo kitty, next time you want to come at me, please come correct. Are you going to eat that?" I asked, happily sitting my ass down while grabbing the donut from off her plate. *Maybe I should give it back. Look like she needs it,* I thought, feeling her bones through her pants leg. *Shit, fuck it! She probably wasn't going to eat it anyway.*

***

"Okay, so I was thinking we could do ivory and gold for the theme colors and my dre—"

"Haley, you know damn well you ain't pure enough to be wearing ivory. Sat that ass down somewhere with that shit." Niamey joked, causing all of us to laugh, although I

115

could tell Haley's was fake. I don't know why she was mad. She knew she used to be a hoe. She'd been hoeing since freshmen year in high school when nigga's started noticing her ass. It was sad but true.

"Nah, let me stop. You're my girl, Haley. This is your day. If you want ivory and gold, then you should get that bih!" she added after the laughter simmered down. I took a sip of my mint julep before nodding in agreement.

"Yeah, girl. An ivory and gold wedding would be bomb," I cosigned. Mariah did one of those little annoying ass snorts as if saying 'this bitch' in response to my statement. Her ass had been throwing shade ever since I got here, but since I was a nice person, I wasn't going to say shit. Today was not about me. As long as she didn't try me like she did earlier, I was going to keep my chill, but let her slip up.

"It would, wouldn't it? Bae and I have already decided we were going to have a beach wedding, like a sunset beach wedding." I see she's going all out.

"You know I love fall, so It's going to be a fall wedding with a white and gold theme!" she gushed. If I didn't know any better, I could've sworn her ass was trying to throw that shit in my face. Haley's ass was a true mess. I didn't give a flying fuck about her and her
116

man's wedding. I wouldn't allow myself to feel some type of way toward them and their marriage. That just made me a petty ass person, and it wasn't a good look on me. I couldn't even feel some type of way toward Messiah anymore. It was about time I put my big girl panties on and moved the fuck on. *Am I fully over him? Nah, but I damn sure ain't about to continue to sweat him. Everything happens for a reason, right?*

God didn't set me up to fail with Messiah just so I could continue to yearn for him like some lovesick puppy. It is what it is. I had to do me and forget Messiah. My feelings for him had to go. He was getting married to Haley, a girl who used to be my sister, but now I didn't know anymore. Things had changed. I had to change. Shit, I needed a change.

CHAPTER 13

Aphrodite Samuels

"Girl, we need to link up sometime. What's your number?" Niamey asked, taking out her phone. She and Asia were dope as fuck. I doubt I would have made it through this damn brunch if it wasn't for Niamey cracking jokes and Asia's chill ass vibes. Haley and her mush mouth friend were feeling very salty this whole entire evening. Shit, I should have been the one mad. Her ass barely asked for my input in helping with her wedding, even though I was supposed to be her "best friend". Like, the fuck? Nonetheless, I cosigned here and there, but for the most part, I just sat back chilling. Mariah still had an attitude, but she knew better than to try me on some dumb shit again.

"Its 407-555-5473." I replied, reciting my number to Niamey. She reminded me of another Samantha but less crazy. I was pretty sure those two would hit it off. I didn't really fuck with a lot of people, but she was a real one. I didn't know how she and Haley were friends. She wasn't anything like her or Mariah, but then again, neither was I. I guess you just gravitate toward people who are different from yourself. To be fair, though, Haley was way chiller when we were younger. Her ego got the best of her. I believe that if I would have met her now in my adult life, I could never associate myself with her. But shit, everything happened for a reason.

"Call me," I spoke before we said our goodbyes and parted ways. *Okay so where to next.* I asked myself as I cruised through the streets of Atlanta. I did need a new pair of shoes. Messiah's aggravating ass killed my Macy's high last Sunday. I rolled my eyes. Macy's it is then.

* * *

"Excuse me. Do you have these in a size six?" I asked a store clerk while holding up a pair of size eight black leather caged heels. I was obsessed with shoes. I didn't really buy heels a lot though, so most of my shoe collection was sneakers.

"I don't know. I'll have to check in the back."

I nodded and waited patiently as she went to search for my shoes. These damn things were seventy dollars, but they would make my legs look good. I don't know when or where I would find the time to wear them, but I would find a way.

A few moments later, she came back with a black box.

"Here you go, ma'am. Anything else?"

I shook my head.

119

"No. I'm good. Thanks!"

I grabbed the box and made my way to the front.

I need a one dance

Got a Hennessy in my hand

One more time 'fore I go

Higher powers taking a hold on me

Ugh! That damn Drake was back at it again with the singing. I was going to trade my Galaxy S6 in for a telegraph six. Get me one of those ancient landlines. I was so done with humanity. Let me stop talking like I was about to jump off a bridge or something and answer this damn phone.

"Aphrodite Samuels speaking. How may I help you?" I asked politely as I stood behind some other woman in one of the checkout aisles. Not too long after my introduction. I heard a familiar ass laugh from the other end. *Damn. Derrick.* Wasn't I supposed to call him? Oh well. I'd had a lot on my mind these past few days.

"You really answer the phone like that. like all the time?"

I couldn't help but suck my teeth at his statement. Why did the way I answered my phone make people laugh all the time? It wasn't even funny.

"Yes, I do. Problem?" I asked with a little attitude. You had to let these people know that just because you're proper doesn't mean you ain't about your issue. I really didn't like when people made fun of how I chose to present myself. It was like making fun of my daddy who raised me to be this way. I didn't play about Avery. I loved my dad to bits. Ugh, now I missed him. I was going to have to give him a call.

"Nah, Goddess. It was just a question. But what are you doing tonight? I want to take you out."

"You want to take me out? Where?" I asked. A girl needed to know what to wear, you know?

"Don't worry about that, Goddess. I got you! Dress casually."

This dude! Why did he feel the need to play with my emotions? He couldn't simply just tell me where we're going? Whatever.

"Alright, you can pick me up at six!" I responded before hanging up on him. Once I finally got up to the cashier, I placed my shoes on the checkout counter along with a few towels and a bottle of Pink Friday by Nicki Minaj. After she scanned my items, I paid for my things and left.

CHAPTER 14

<u>Aphrodite Samuels</u>

"Don't get it twisted. You were just another nigga on the hit list, trying to fix your inner issues with a bad bitch. Didn't they tell that I was a savage?"

I sang Rihanna's "Needed Me" as I got dressed for my date with Derrick. It was now 5:30, and Derrick was coming to pick me up at six. Samantha wasn't here to help me this time, but I could manage on my own.

"You needed me. Ooh, you needed me."

I twerked a little as I put on my mascara. I was standing in front of my full-length mirror, putting on my makeup. Derrick said to dress casually, so for tonight, I decided to dress in a gray crop top and legging set from Fashion Nova, along with a pair of all-white Adidas superstars.

I painted my lips with a mocha colored lip stain before giving my outfit one last full body analysis. *Girl, we look good as fuck.* I mentally nodded in agreement at my statement. I had that glow thing going for me. My hair was cooperating, and I had a face beat for the gods. Shit, I was doing the damn thing. I laughed at my overconfident attitude before checking the time. It read 5:50, ten minutes before Derrick arrived. I was already done getting dressed, so I decided to watch *Good times* for a bit in the living room.

***

Oh my God. No, he didn't. I shook my head and looked at Derrick who was looking at me with a knowing look on his face.

"No, you didn't!" I said, grinning like a mad man. This man had just pulled up to Dave and Busters. I hadn't been here in ages. I was always working, and it seemed like I never had time to do things like this. A teacher's job never really stopped at the bell. It was a lot of time spent on planning and grading work when it came to my free time. Yes, I was a kindergarten teacher, but I liked my lessons to be fun and well planned. That shit took some time and a lot of effort. Derrick shrugged.

"Why not hit up Dave and Busters where a kid can be a kid?"

To that, I laughed.

"And here I thought you were about to go all out for a girl. And FYI, that's Chuck E. Cheese," I said, but to be honest, I was grinning hard as fuck now. What could I say? I was a kid at heart. He shrugged once more.

"And..." he simply stated. I rolled my eyes.

123

"Whatever, let's go!" I spoke, slamming his door a bit too harshly due to my excitement.

"Don't go slamming my door, girl! Did she hurt you, baby?" he asked as he felt up his car. I laughed.

"Dude, you're stupid. But for real though, let's go. I want to get me something to eat. Ooh, bruh, I'm about to play every game they got. Shoot, I might even make a bet or two. Nah, them wings though, I'm going get me some of them forea— what?" I asked Derrick, who seemed to be watching my every move, making me feel some type of way at the look he was giving me. Lord Jesus, I needed some Nay right now! If I was anything like Samantha, boy, I swear.

"I like this side of you; very energetic, peaceful, and most of all, happy. I'm glad I could be the one to put that smile on your face."

"U-uh."

I blushed. *What the hell has this man done to me*, I thought, feeling my heartbeat ten times faster than it had been before. I needed to calm myself before I did something I might regret later.

I shook my head to clear my thoughts before smacking my teeth. "Yeah, whatever. Let's just eat and fuck some shit up," I spoke, referring to the games on that

124

last note. Derrick laughed and followed me as I headed into the building. Once we were seated at the restaurant, we ordered our food before deciding to play a game of pool.

"You don't even know it, but I'm a pro when it comes to pool," I said in all seriousness. Derrick laughed before nodding.

"Alright, bet."

I shrugged. Ol' dude must not have known, but pool was my shit.

"Bet."

***

"I'm dead ass. It was me, my brother, Khalil, and two cousins, Jamal and Shemar. I had to try to outrun all three of their asses, plus some dogs. I knew I should have never gotten my ass in that car. I got a major ass whooping after my mama bailed me out of juvie."

I laughed as I watched Derrick wince after he mentioned the whooping he had received after him, his brother, and cousins decided they were going to go on a joyride in a stolen vehicle. Apparently, it was his cousin, Jamal's, idea, and they just went along with it. It had been a good twenty minutes into our date, and right now, we were eating and telling old ass whooping memories.

125

"And don't think I forgot, Goddess. You owe me."

My mood immediately went sorrowful as I thought about earlier events. Long story short, I lost in pool, and now I owed him one.

"You cheated."

"Really? How, Sway?"

"I don't know, but you did."

I shrugged, crossing my hands over my chest and pouting in the process. Ain't no way in hell I had lost. Derrick laughed at my childishness, staring at me with this intense emotion as if he could see inside my soul, causing my stomach to do backflips. Where was my Nay when I needed it?

"Is my goddess mad? Don't hate the player, baby. You'll get it next time."

I rolled my eyes at the patronizing tone of his voice as he tried to reason with me. *Ol' cheating ass*! I kissed my teeth and rolled my eyes once more.

"Who said I wanted to go out with you again? I don't like cheaters," I said, giving him a little attitude, low-key lying. Derrick nodded before getting up and coming to my side of the booth. *The fuck is he doing*, I questioned, eyeing him from the side as he started getting closer and closer to me.

126

"Oh really?"

I nodded, trying to keep up my front, but baby girl was over here feeling some type of way. I inhaled a bit and shuddered at the citrus cologne he had on. Lord knows I loved a man who could pick a scent. He smelled like Versace Pour-Homme, an expensive ass bottle of liquid that I wouldn't pay for myself, but it smelled good.

"I must smell really good. You over there inhaling deep as fuck." Derrick joked, causing me to roll my eyes before pushing him away.

"Nah, you're just smelling yourself. You ain't even all that. Fawk you mean?" I spoke, trying not to smile. Derrick chuckled that panty dropper type chuckle as he pulled me closer to his body. With Dite being Dite, my immature ass chose to squirm, despite the fact that my body was telling me no.

"Don't nobody want your cooties!" I said childishly, feigning repulsion.

"Girl, you know you love my cooties," he spoke lowly in my ear, sending chills all up and down my body. I was over here on that Rihanna shit; talk that talk to me. He wasn't even saying anything necessarily sexual, but I was slowly getting turned on.

"N-Nah, I'm good,"

Really, Dite? I'm good? You acting like he asked you did you want some chips or something.

I mentally face palmed myself. The fuck was wrong with me?

"Goddess, I ain't ask how you doing. I said you know you love my cooties, and I'm not hearing any disagreement. Now give your man some sugar!"

Your man, I mused with a small smile on my face. Did he really said that? Maybe he hadn't even meant it like that. *Let's not get ahead of ourselves here. I did that before and look where that got me.* Man, I needed to stop mixing the two situations. These were two different people and two different personalities. It wasn't the same. *Let me stop getting all up in my head on this one.* I thought before replying.

"Like I said, I'm good. I don't want your cooties."

"Please?"

"No, you've been bad today."

"What I do?"

"I don't know, but I'll think of something."

"I just want one kiss."

"Why?"

"I want to taste the melons."

128

"So you're Martin now?"

"If that's what it takes, you can be my Gina."

"So I have a big head now?"

"I didn't even want to say anything, but you said it."

"Whatever!"

"Can I still get that kiss, though?"

"Nah, I don't like you."

"Why are you lying?"

"I'm not."

Derrick and I went back and forth for a while, completely ignoring the fact that we were in a restaurant full of people who were probably looking at us like we were crazy. Eventually, we both busted out laughing over how stupid our asses were being. To be real, this was the chillest date I had ever been on. Messiah and I didn't necessarily go on dates, and I was Omar's little secret.

"I'm dead ass, though. Can I have a kiss?"

Kiss 'em, Kiss 'em!

Oh my God! I rolled my eyes playfully before giving him a little peck on the cheek. Derrick gave me that 'don't play with it' look.

"Now you know damn well that wasn't what I was talking about! Kiss me like you mean it because I know you want it."

129

I rolled my eyes and kissed my teeth before giving Derrick my full attention.

"I don't know where your lips have been. I ain't trying to get no types of di——"

I was caught off guard by Derrick's lips. His tongue grazed the bottom of my lip, asking me to let him in, but Dite's ass just had to be difficult. I kept my mouth shut just to tease his ass. I'm guessing Derrick didn't like my teasing very much. He gave my sides a pinch, and Dite, being so damn ticklish, gasped. This gave Derrick the opportunity to slip his tongue into my mouth. Our asses were going at it, completely ignoring the fact that we were still in a public place. I knew I had to stop this. Shit was getting too heated, and I was two seconds away from being laid on this table.

Reluctantly, I pulled away from the kiss. Derrick licked his lips, eyeing me up and down with those bedroom eyes.

"I was wrong. You taste like peaches."

CHAPTER 15

<u>Aphrodite Samuels</u>

"Whatever, Derrick. I know you cheated!"

"Really, Goddess? You're still on that?"

"Ya damn Skippy!" I responded matter-of-factly to Derrick. We were currently on the phone video chatting, and he just had to bring up the favor I owed him from that bet we'd made two weeks ago.

We had been calling or video chatting nonstop since then because we both were so busy, and me being me, nine times out of ten, I was always asleep. Everything had been pretty chill thus far, and I could honestly say I was happy. Despite the fact that we aren't a couple yet, I could definitely say Derrick was a good man. He was always able to keep a smile on my face, and every time we spoke, I forgot about all my worries. Messiah kind of took the back seat in my mind, but I wasn't going to lie. The love was still there. He was my first love, and that could never change, but I realized that I had to stop putting my life on hold for him.

Haley hadn't been bugging me about her wedding, and that was a plus as well. Shit, my ass was probably just going to show up, eat, and then leave. Free food was free food. Fuck the marriage! I was going to keep it pushing.

"Speaking of that deal, I think I want to cash in that favor."

Bruh! I kissed my teeth and rolled my eyes in annoyance. *Ol' cheating ass*, I thought with a shake of my head. I didn't need him messing with my mood right now. *Ain't nobody trying to do anything for his ass! I just want to sleep and eat.*

"Awe. Goddess. Don't be like that. I promise it won't be anything embarrassing or demeaning. I would never do that to you."

Derrick smirked, using his trademark panty dropper smirk, making the kid feel weak. Boy, I just might give into my inner hoe desires. Lately, I'd been fiendin', and that thirst wasn't a good look on me.

"Mmm hmm, but I ain't no punk, so what you want me to do?"

I watched his smirk turn into a full-blown smile, and I instantly became scared. This couldn't be good.

***

"Really, dude? Are you serious?" I asked with a roll of my eyes as I watched Derrick rummage through my cupboards, looking for God knows what. This fool had

132

the audacity to waltz his ass into my home and tell me that his favor was that he wanted me to cook him dinner. All that beating around the bush was just to tell me he wanted to eat. I could've gone to Ming Li's and gotten him a plate of honey chicken and rice for cheap, but nah. He wanted me to cook. I shook my head at him.

I had just gone grocery shopping the other day, and someone was already trying to eat up my food. I swear, the nerve of some people these days didn't make any sense.

"What? Mama said if she can't cook, don't bring her home. If you going to be with a nigga on some real shit, you better know how to season chicken and boil some rice. We don't play 'round here! Plus, a nigga been working hard all week trying to get my business together. The least you can do is cook your man some food."

Derrick gave me that 'better get to it' look. Who the fuck said I wanted to be with him long term anyway? He was just getting way too ahead of himself. He wasn't even all that.

"Boy, bye. I could've just took you to Mickey D's and let you cash out on the dollar menu for that." I spoke, rolling my eyes as I folded my hands across my chest. Yes, I was giving him a little attitude, but truth be told, I

133

was no housewife! I could cook and clean, but he better not be thinking this was going to be a daily thing if we did decide to push whatever was going on between us further.

"Girl, ain't nobody want none of that horse meat they call a burger! There ain't no dollar menu anyway, charging damn near two dollars for a motherfucking soda. You can get a damn Polar pop from Circle K for seventy-nine cents. Fuck they got going on?"

I laughed at Derrick's little rant. He was spitting nothing but facts. McDonald's was tripping with them prices, and maybe their meat wasn't all 100%, but the shit was food though, so fuck it! If I was hungry, I was going to eat, point blank.

"Whatever, Derrick. I got you though! Go sit down somewhere, and you better not come in my kitchen until I tell you to."

I shooed him, waving my hand dismissively out of my kitchen. I was hungry too, so I might as well cook. Lord knows it had been a good little minute since I'd made an actual meal in this kitchen.

He kissed his teeth before walking out of the kitchen and into the living room. A few moments later, I heard the TV click on and the voice of Martin Lawrence telling

134

Pam and them to get to stepping. I laughed a little as I took out two packages of spare ribs to defrost while I boiled the water for the mac and cheese. Your girl had been craving some ribs, and I'd been wanting to try making Cola ribs. It was a recipe I saw on Pinterest a while ago. Knowing me, when I actually did cook, I loved experimenting with new recipes and shit like I was some type of iron chef, Gordon Ramsey or something.

I grabbed two boxes of elbow pasta from my pantry before pouring them into the boiling water. I then went into my room and grabbed a two-liter bottle of Coca Cola to make my Cola sauce for the ribs. Yes, I kept snacks and shit in my room. Knowing Samantha's thieving greedy ass, if I didn't, all my fudge brownies, oatmeal pies, and soda would be gone. It was stupid, but it seemed to work.

"Goddess, are you done yet? I'm hungry!"

I shook my head. Lord Jesus, give me the strength.

CHAPTER 16

<u>Aphrodite Samuels</u>

"Goddess, if you don't gon' somewhere. This shit is good. Who taught you to cook like this?" Derrick asked, shocked at the fact that I could actually throw down in the kitchen. I laughed and shook my head at his amazement. I mean, I knew I could cook, but it wasn't all that he was making it out to be. He had the BBQ sauce dripping from the corner of his mouth, looking like a damn child. *I can't with this man,* I thought. I smiled.

"It ain't even all that serious, but I taught myself how to cook. My dad can't cook for shit, so I had to come up with something. I couldn't continue to eat fruity pebbles all day."

I shrugged it off. Every day in the house with Avery we had cereal for breakfast, lunch, and dinner. Being that fruity pebbles was our favorite, it was a staple in our household. Eventually, I got tired of eating cereal for breakfast, so I decided to try to create pancakes for myself. It was a fail, but as time went on, I got better at it. Since I stayed watching *Food Network* as a child, I always felt the need to want to experiment in the kitchen, hence why I can cook now.

"See, I know I caught me a good one! Up here whipping up biscuits and shit like you're Paula Deen," Derrick voiced with a mouth full of food. I reached over my little black dinette table and popped his left cheek before wagging my hands in a scolding manner at him.

"Close your mouth, ya little nasty!" I said, mimicking Raven Symone from *That's So Raven*. He gave me that 'you tried it' look as he started smacking like one of them ratchet stale weave wearing, gum smacking girls that I used to go to high school with back in the day.

"Firstly, ain't nothing little 'bout your boy. Secondly, you know you like my nasty."

He smirked, pulling his bottom lip between his lips.

He swear he's cute. Rolling my eyes, I coughed to clear up my mild thirst before responding.

"Boy, bye! And I hope you know you cleaning these dishes. I cooked. You clean."

I shrugged. I'll be damned if I slave over a hot stove for a good hour and then have to go and wash some dishes. I hated washing dishes with a passion, which was why I hadn't been cooking as much lately.

"Aight, bet."

***

"What's up, bitch?

"Hey, hoe."

"Why you call me?"

I kissed my teeth. It was just like my daddy to be so rude toward his only child. Let me stop bullshitting. I loved my Avery. My daddy was my best friend, and I his, which was why we spoke the way we did with each other. It was nothing personal. It was just how we were.

"Really, Daddy. You tell me to answer the phone like I have sense, but then hit me with a 'what's up, bitch'. You make me cry!" I pouted with a roll of my eyes. I could hear my dad kiss his teeth as if saying 'this child' before he replied.

"Girl, I saw your big ass head pop up on my screen, ruining my cake session with Jackie from down the street."

Bruh, no. Chill. Ain't nobody trying to hear about his sexcapades! I just couldn't with him and the visuals. Just nasty.

"Really, Daddy. I thought you loved me? Ain't I more important than some lil' booty, anyway?"

"Girl, you're grown. Now get off my pho—"

"Wait!"

My dad sighed.

138

"Girl, what?"

I swear I got no love from this man. I pouted. "I miss you, Daddy," I spoke in a small innocent tone as I cradled my cell phone between my right cheek and shoulder. I was such a daddy's girl. I couldn't stand being away from my wodie for so long without speaking to him for so long. I didn't know how I had lasted up until this point. Aphrodite without Avery was like you without oxygen.

"And tell me why you gave Haley my number?" I asked him, remembering I had never called him about that whole Haley incident.

"That ain't none of my business. That's your best friend. Speaking of which, how the fuck did she get my number anyway? Ol' stalking ass, I knew she wanted me. That lil' girl nasty. She tried to flex that itty-bitty booty when she came over to use the pool that one time. That girl ain't slick. Jailbait as—"

"Avery!" I snapped, cutting off my daddy from continuing his little rant about Haley. Ever since we were freshmen in high school, my dad would always pick up on the changes in Haley, thus he voiced his opinions about her all the time. He didn't really like the new Haley, and to be honest, I didn't like her either, but I continued to support and be there for her.

139

"Daddy, she's getting married."

"That poor man."

I laughed.

"I'm dead serious, daddy, and guess what?"

"I ain't playing this guessing game with you."

Just hurt my feelings why don't you, I thought, shaking my head at my dad's attitude toward me. Maybe I should have let him get his dose of sugar and told him this shit later. That man had an attitude.

"Whatever, but she's getting married to Messiah," I told him. My dad knew about Messiah ever since he'd caught him in my apartment back when he would make unannounced visits just to see if I was still on my shit. Messiah and I weren't doing anything, but that ain't stop my dad from giving that 'fuck with me if you want to' daddy look. I inwardly laughed, remembering when he told Messiah 'whatever you do to my daughter, you doing to me'. He said he wanted Messiah to visualize him every time he even thought about sleeping with me or something. No chill whatsoever. We all knew how that story went, but I reassured him that we were just "friends". *Friends my ass*, I thought sarcastically.

"Oh, you mean that Michael Ealy wannabe? I knew that boy was dumb. What is he doing with Thottiana?

140

Probably caught all types of diseases. You know she gets around."

My daddy stayed talking shit. Unlike me, he had no filter which was crazy because he was the one who had raised me to be the woman I was today.

"You sound like a female. She asked me to be her maid of honor."

I heard a cackle, snort-like laugh come from the other end of the phone as well as the sound of someone dry heaving, causing me to frown. My daddy kind of had an idea that Messiah and I were a bit more than friends. He just didn't know how serious we were.

"Want me to beat his ass?"

He laughed, causing me to roll my eyes. He found this shit funny.

"Bye, Avery!"

"Wait, I'm sor—"

CLICK! I sighed. I needed new people in my life.

CHAPTER 16

<u>Aphrodite Samuels</u>

"So did Derrick finally dust those cobwebs off your pum-pum?"

I kissed my teeth and rolled my eyes at the foolishness that Samantha decided to voice. I honestly didn't know what was wrong with this child. I swear dick was all she thought about. I knew she meant no harm. It was just who she was, but she needed to find some chill. I knew I was still young, but that didn't mean I needed to live wild. Free maybe, but wild? Nah, that wasn't for me. The only time I'd ever allowed myself to let loose in that way was with Messiah, and like I said, that wasn't something I was trying to go through again. I wanted to have a meaningful and respectable relationship with a man before I gave myself to him.

"No, Samantha. We just chilled," I replied, sipping on my watermelon Arizona as I watched the waves crash against the shoreline. Since Samantha thought we needed some best friend time, she decided we were going to the beach. Shit, my ass wasn't complaining. I needed a little sun in my life. Plus, all I did was work, sleep, eat, and repeat, so I needed a change. The sun felt mighty good on my skin too.

142

I grinned softly and looked toward my bestie who was currently trying to build a sandcastle with a pail and shovel she had stolen from some little kid a few yards away from us. I shook my head at my best friend. Times like this, I realized why Haley was never my true best friend. We were just too different. Granted, Sam and I weren't one in the same either, but we clicked on a whole other level. She didn't try to hide who she was in front of me or anyone else, which was why I respected her. She was childish, but for her, it worked. Haley felt the need to change herself to fit the other girls our age, but Sam, she was still the same childish ass outspoken individual she had been since the first day I'd met her. She respected me for me, and unless I was in the wrong, had my back whenever. She was truly my best friend and sister for life.

"Man, you gay!" Samantha spoke up, mimicking Riley from *The Boondocks*, causing me to laugh before gulping down the rest of my drink.

"How, Sway?" I pondered with a roll of my eyes, tossing the can aside. Sam shrugged.

"You keep staring at me, girl! I know I'm fine. I'm my mama's daughter, but that doesn't make it okay for you to try to steal my face, just hard down gawking at a nigga," she rambled, giving me that 'what are you doing' look. I

143

laughed again. I could never take this child seriously. *Don't nobody want her! I prefer mine built like Chyna. Fawk she mean?*

I laughed. Let me stop playing. I shook my head to clear my thoughts. "Why you always spacing out on me, Dite? You know what? I'm done!"

With that being said, she got up and left, stomping away. Okay. I shrugged, deciding to take a walk myself.

***

"What flavor?"

"Piña Colada, please." I told the man who was selling shaved ice on the boardwalk. Your girl was over here hungry, and Samantha was nowhere to be found, which was stupid because she was the one who had invited me to the damn beach! Sometimes, I couldn't with her, man.

I watched the Hispanic man put together my icy treat.

"Here you go, ma'am!" he spoke, handing me the cup. I smiled, thanking him as I took it before handing him two dollars. I bid him a farewell before leaving. I munched on the frosty concoction, making my way down the boardwalk. I must say, this thing tasted better than it looked. It actually tasted like a Piña Colada drink.

I hummed a soft melody as I licked the ice off the spoon, trying to refrain from moaning. This shit was that

144

good, man. I swear. See, I didn't really fuck with ice cream, but I loved shaved ice, sorbet and gelato. Samantha said it was the same thing, but it wasn't.

"Bambie!"

Bruh, say it ain't so. I groaned. *Damn. Messiah!* I smacked my teeth and rolled my eyes, deciding that I wasn't going to turn around. I continued to make my way down the boardwalk, ignoring Messiah's calls. I would not entertain him today.

So you say... I'll wait.

I mentally rolled my eyes at myself. Where was my chill, dude?

"Bambie, girl, I know you hear me!"

This dude!

I kept walking, ignoring the looks I received from some people due to Messiah screaming after me. Ugh, the nerve! I snacked on my icy as I started back humming again. I was going to ignore Messiah as much as I possibly could until he got the picture that I wasn't going to play his games anymore. I felt a hand reach out and latch onto my kimono cover-up.

"Damn, your ass is fast!"

That damn Messiah! God be playing with me, boy, I swear.

145

"Get off of me," I groaned, annoyed by Messiah's presence. Why couldn't he just leave me alone? I just wanted to have a peaceful beach day, but I couldn't even do that. *Why, God? Why?* I sucked my teeth. The day was just going great, and then this shit happened. I just couldn't catch a break, could I?

I felt the weight on my cover up drop, causing me to sigh in relief before turning around to face Messiah. Rolling my eyes, I scanned Messiah from head to toe and frowned. Why the hell did he have to have his shirt off? Lord knows that six pack was deadly. I couldn't, man, and it looked like he had just stepped out of the water.

You know what? Stop it, Dite! We ain't gon' do this today.

I rolled my eyes.

"Bye, Messiah," I spoke dismissively before turning around. I heard him suck in a breath, feeling his hard gaze on my behind.

"Damn," he mumbled lowly, but I could clearly hear him. The nerve! I sighed, fixin' to head back to the spot Samantha and I were occupying.

"Wait," he spoke up, latching onto my wrist. I looked at him like he had lost his mind, but I couldn't lie and say

I didn't get that tingly feeling where his arms were placed on me.

Damn you, Messiah!

"Man, what?" I asked, aggravated. I already knew that if he was here, Haley wasn't too far behind. Lord knows I didn't have time for her shit today. Where the fuck was Samantha when you needed her?

"I just want to talk. I miss you, Bambie," he spoke sincerely, but I just couldn't bring myself to believe those words. I couldn't, and I wouldn't be sucked into his lies anymore. No matter how slick his talk game was, I wouldn't allow him the opportunity to have my heart again. That wasn't fair to Derrick, and that damn sure wasn't fair to me. He and Haley could go play house for all I cared. I was done.

"Mmm hmm. That's really nice that you feel that way. I have to go now," I spoke again, trying to pry my arm out of his grasp but to no avail.

"Messiah," I growled, tugging his arm again. I just wanted to leave and get me another icy before taking a little dip in the water.

"Please?"

I sighed as our eyes found each other. His beautifully familiar warm greenish hazel orbs bore into mine. I

147

looked away. *Not again, Dite*, I mentally whispered, but it was already too late.

Messiah Lafayette

"Fine..."

A huge joker like grin took over my face at the sound of her reply. I was low-key excited, but I had to play it cool. I smiled down at her, watching as she mugged the ground. Damn, she was cute as fuck. *Nah. Siah. Stop thinking like that,* I told myself, mentally shaking my head at myself. Dite wasn't my girl. I couldn't be thinking shit like that toward her.

"I mean, are we just gonna stand up here or..." Dite trailed off, sounding annoyed. I honestly didn't know who she thought she was catching an attitude with. I don' told her that attitude shit didn't work for her. I knew this shit sounded corny as fuck, but she was too beautiful to be having an attitude like that. It just wasn't a good look on her.

I nodded.

"Aight, Bambie. Keep at it. You already know I don't like that attitude shit on you, girl. But on a serious note, I really do miss you," I spoke sincerely, hoping she could hear how genuine my words were. I didn't necessarily understand what had gone wrong with us, and I knew us not keeping in contact led up to us acting like strangers now, but I really did miss my Bambie. I wanted us to be

149

cool again. despite that. I missed my best friend. I missed our talks and how we used to kick it back in the day. Bambie was my rock. and I needed that.

Dite let out a little scoff. as if saying 'yeah right' as she shook her head.

"That's cool. Is that all?" she asked, seemingly impatient. *Still got that damn attitude I see.* I smacked my teeth. pulling her to face me. I watched her frown before rolling her eyes, causing me to let out a breath. If this girl don't gon' somewhere with that shit. I was about to smack some sense into her ass if she didn't stop this petty shit.

"I'm gon' need you to stop with that attitude shit, aight? Now come kick it with me, like old times," I demanded. not really giving her an opportunity to say yes or no. because I had already started to pull her alongside me down the boardwalk.

"Stop playing with me. Binky! Let me go," she protested as I continued to steer her in the direction of my little set up with some of my people. I ignored her.

"Where are we going?"

She sighed. I guess she finally realized that I wasn't taking no for an answer. Like I said, I was gon' get my best friend back.

150

"I want you to meet some people." I spoke coolly, giving a slight shrug while I looked down at her. She had that cute ass little pout on her face that she always got when she was either confused or thinking heavily about something. At the moment, I would say she was both. Here I was, dragging her to God knows where, and here she was, trying to decide if she wanted to give your boy a chance or just keep it pushing. Hopefully, once we started kickin' it, she'd bounce back to the old Bambie, just down to cool it whenever.

"Just irritating, man. You're lucky I'm nice." she spoke, smacking her teeth. Her eyes looked up to lock with mine. Her eyes held a spark in them, a spark that I had missed so much. Damn, she was beau—*Nah, Siah. Stop thinking shit like that! She's just your best friend. Haley is your girl.* I had to remember that. I said nothing in reply to her statement and continued to guide her to the spot. Not even twenty minutes later, we finally arrived at our destination.

"I know damn well that ain't who I think it is! Juicy Fruit, is that you, girl!" Landon's ol' loud ass shouted, causing everybody to look at us. I smacked my teeth, *ol' loudmouth ass.* I kissed my teeth and side-eyed Landon. *Who the fuck is Juicy Fruit?*

151

Just as I was about to ask this dumb ass fool who that was, Bambie pulled out of my grasp and went to go hug this ugly ass nigga. On my soul, they'd better have a good ass explanation because I swear...

"Chunky, boy, your ass don' glowed up! Ain't so chunky anymore. You look good."

"Wait a minute. Y'all two know each other?" I asked, scratching my head. I was legit confused as fuck. Don't tell me these niggas used to date. I mean, Dite couldn't have gone for this ugly ass nigga, could she? Dite and that ugly nigga laughed like it was just the funniest shit I was saying.

"Of course. He's Haley's cousin."

Dite smiled up at the fool. *Bruh, I should've known that shit.* I keep forgetting Haley and Dite went way back, but why the fuck was he looking at her like that? Ol' ugly ass smirked, licking his lips as he eyed up my Bambie. I frowned. Why the fuck had she chosen to wear that damn bathing suit? She knew damn well those curves had niggas losing their minds. I couldn't, man. He'd better tighten up, though. I was not trying to go to jail today. That nigga did not want these problems, swear.

"Yep, we go way back on Peach Street. Juicy Fruit used to be my lil' baby."

152

Why did this nigga keep calling her Juicy Fruit? Dite rolled her eyes.

"Lil' boy, bye! You know you were and still are too young for me," she spoke, causing me to smirk inwardly. *Nigga just got that ass shooed! Better sit his baby ass down somewhere. My Bambie doesn't want that.*

"Girl, I'm a grown ass man now! Nineteen and counting, baby." Ol'dumbass smirked like that was going to make a difference.

Bambie rolled her eyes. "Yeah, okay... I'm good on you, though. I got me somebody."

Pause. She said what now?

Aphrodite Samuels

"Shut your ass up, Landon, before I call Tomi and tell her your ass over here trying to mac and shit!" I heard someone shout, causing the smile to immediately leave Chunky's face and a frown to form on my own. I smacked my teeth at the nerve of this child. A nigga had one good glow up, and now he thought he was a player. One thing I hated was a lying, cheating ass individual.

"You lucky I ain't trying to fight, Chunky. You know how I feel about that cheating shit," I spoke, scolding him. I eyed Chunky as he let his head fall in shame. Since Haley and I were like sisters once upon a time, she and her people knew about my dad's situation with my mom and how that affected him, so they knew I hated cheaters.

"What y'all over here doing?" I heard the same voice who called Chunky out say, seeming closer than before. Landon was soon pushed out the way, and in his place stood a sexy piece of dark chocolate, over there looking like a snicker bar. *Let me stop.*

"Oh shit. Who thi—Aphro?" he asked as his eyes widened.

"You look good, girl!" he added. I eyed him, confused. How the fuck did he know me?

154

"Umm, do I know you?" I asked, trying not to sound rude. I honestly did not know if I knew this man, but apparently, he knew me. Ol' dude smirked.

"Damn, so you remember Siah's ol' fat headed ass, but you don't remember me? Oh, okay. It's me, Tremaine AKA Trey AKA that fuck nigga that hit you," he replied. I blinked a few times, trying to scrape my brain for that name before finally coming to realization. Now I knew where I knew him from, UGA. He was Messiah's friend. I'd met him after me and Messiah's first encounter at the basketball court. He was the one who actually threw the ball my way. He and I became cool after he apologized of course, but like Messiah and Haley, we lost touch after graduation. Nodding, I smiled.

"Oh, hi. How have you been?" I asked, earning a little smirk from him as he gave me a onceover.

"I'm good. Shit, great actually, but you?"

He paused, eyeing me up and down again before continuing.

"In the words of J Cole, can make an old man get his glasses, make Wesley pay his taxes," he finished, rapping the lyrics to J Cole's "Can't Get Enough." I laughed a little and noticed Trey giving Messiah a look.

"Aight, that's enou—"

155

"Damn! That sure as hell ain't Haley." I heard, causing me to whip around to face two other fine brothas walking toward us. Lord Jesus, I was surrounded by all this fine chocolate. *I can't, man.*

"Before y'all nigga's get too close, this is Dite. Dite these are my boys, Safari, Drake, and Quinton."

Messiah introduced us, pointing to each of them as he said their names. I gave them a small hi and a wave while watching as they got closer to us. They continued to eye my body, making me feel a little weird, so I tugged the little cover-up thingy tighter around my body.

"Aye, stop looking at her like that!" Messiah snapped. All the other boys laughed, which seemed to irk Messiah even more by the evident mug on his face.

"Who's afraid of the big bad wolf? Nah though, don't worry, Sy. That's all you." Quinton spoke, causing me to roll my eyes in distaste. *Just who the fuck do they think I am? Talking 'bout some 'Sy, that's all you.' Boy, bye!*

I kissed my teeth, folding my arms across my chest.

"Last time I checked, Haley was all Messiah. Don't try me!" I snapped. I felt like they were accusing me of being Messiah's sideline, and a sideline was something that I wasn't. Safari nodded, raising his hands up in defense.

156

"I apologize for my gender's rude behavior. You look too good for Sy anyway. What's your sign?"

What the fuck?

"Pisces," I answered, confused as to where he was going with this. I was not about that astrology and zodiac sign shit. A smirk took over Safari's face before he responded.

"Well I'm a Cancer, and you know what they say about us Pisces and Cancers when we get together? The se—fuck, Siah! Damn! You could've killed me!" Safari all but shouted, rubbing the front his neck. Messiah did some ninja shit and karate chopped the dude right in his throat. I knew that shit must've hurt. Messiah shrugged like fuck the charge as he gave Safari the meanest mug ever, ol' sensitive ass. I laughed.

"Well, it was nice meeting you guys. I have to go back to my spot before Sam starts tripping. See you guys around!"

I smiled, waving before making my way back to me and Sam's spot.

CHAPTER 17

Aphrodite Samuels

"So let me get this straight. You were surrounded by all that glorious melanin and didn't bother to bring me back a Hershey's bar? Really, Aphro? That's what we're doing now?" Samantha sputtered in confusion after I had finished telling her what happened after her ass went missing a while ago. We were still at the beach, and I was helping her bury herself in the sand since that's what she wanted to do. I didn't know why, but eh. That was none of my business. I shrugged.

"I mean, didn't anybody tell you to storm off," I spoke, nonchalantly. I watched Samantha roll her eyes.

"Just rude! But aye, ol' dude was jealous." she said, causing me to eye her curiously. Who the fuck was she talking about? Chunky? I mean, sure. It still seemed like he had a slight crush on me, but he did have some girl named Tomi already, so I mean, why would he be jealous?

"I see you're still dumb. I'm talking about Messiah, girl. Damn!"

The fuck? I eyed Samantha as if she were crazy, which she honestly was because there was no way that

Messiah would be jealous over me. That dude had a whole bitch out here.

"Did somebody give you some edibles while you were gone? You are acting like you on something," I asked, feeling a bit worried. Samantha must've been on something because clearly, she wasn't thinking correctly. Sam rolled her eyes.

"Girl, boo! Check it. He didn't want anybody else looking at you, and he got mad when that Love and Hip Hop nigga tried to come on to you. Don't that seem odd to you?" she asked, staring at me as if I was just the dumbest person ever. What the hell was she talking about? I mean, we were best friends at some point in time, so the protectiveness was understandable.

I scoffed. "Stop being stupid, Samantha. That man ain't thinking 'bout me!" I spoke, dismissively. Messiah had his lady, and her name was Haley. He didn't want me.

***

Messiah Lafayette

Two hours later

"So how you know Juicy Fruit?" Landon's retarded ass asked, eyeing me suspiciously. I side-eyed this dude. The fuck did he care so much? That was none of his business, and why the fuck did he keep calling my Bambie Juicy Fruit? On my soul, this fool was 'bout to get dropped on his neck.

"Nigga, who the fuck is Juicy Fruit?" Quinton asked, just as confused as the rest of them niggas. Shit, I wanted to know the story behind this Juicy Fruit shit my damn self.

"Oh, my bad. Y'all know her by Aphrodite. Juicy Fruit AKA my baby?"

Ol' dumb ass smirked. Trey snorted, looking from me to Landon. None of my people really knew Dite or what she was to me except Trey. We both knew that I'd had Bambie first. This little nigga was just wishing. I continued to mean mug this goofy looking ass nigga. He was lucky he was Haley's cousin. I didn't even like that nigga, to be honest. He was too damn playful, and I wasn't with that fufu shit.

"Aye, why you call her Juicy Fruit? Is it because that ass is jui—"

160

Before Drake could finish his sentence, I had popped his ass in the back of the head quick as fuck.

"What the fuck, man? Damn!"

"See, I knew you and ol' girl got something going on. Damn near almost killed a nigga earlier behind her ass, and now you 'bout to give this nigga brain damage. So, what is she? Your mistress?" Safari joked, causing all these nosy ass niggas to look at me.

"Bruh, not my Juicy Fruit! Really? And you cheating on my cousin?" ol' dumb ass said.

"Nigga, you mad or nah?" Trey asked in response to Landon's statement.

"Nah, I mean, Juicy Fruit is... shit, juicy. And Haley might be my cousin, but we all know she's a hoe. With that being said, I give you my blessing."

Nigga, what? Trey smacked his teeth.

"Blessing? Nigga, you ain't that girl daddy. The fuck he needs your blessing for?" he asked. Hell, I wanted to know my damn self. I mean, who exactly did this 'I-belong-in-the-human-centipede' looking ass nigga think he is? Nobody was cheating on Haley!

"Nah, what I really want to know is if you really smashing shawty?"

Bruh. I smacked my teeth.

161

"Dite ain't even like that. She's just a friend," I spoke, causing all of their asses to laugh.

"And you say she's just a friend," Drake's extra gay ass started singing, causing these hyena ass niggas to laugh harder. A nigga felt like Kevin Hart right now and was gon' be selling out shows at Busch Gardens in a minute. Safari smacked his teeth.

"Friend? Oh okay. So you don't mind if I—"

"Nigga, what?" I spoke up, cutting him off. I knew damn well this fool wasn't stupid. Better shut that shit down right now, 'cause it wasn't gon' happen. Bruh had me fucked up!

"See! If she's just a friend, why are you catching an attitude? I mean, if she ain't for you, can she at least be for me?"

This nigga...

"Fuck out of here with that shit! Plus, didn't she say she had a dude already?" I countered, feeling slightly unnerved at the thought of her and that other dude. I think she said his name was Sam or some shit, probably short for Samuel, ol' lame ass nigga.

"Aight, y'all leave this nigga and his just a friend ass alone. Nah, real talk. Let me holla at you for a minute, Sy," Trey spoke, looking at me like he knew something

162

was up. I wasn't trying to get into my feelings at the moment, but I knew Trey was being dead ass. That was my nigga since day one, and I knew he was gon' always look out for a nigga, even when I wasn't trying to hear it.

Damn, I sound like a female, I thought with a grimace. I sighed and hopped up out of my seat before stepping out with Trey.

"What's up with you, bruh?"

I shrugged.

"Shit, nothing."

"Don't give me that mess. What happened?" Trey asked again with a smack of his teeth. I sighed, stroking my chin hairs. *This kid! You know what? Fuck it.*

"I just want my Bambie back... none of that extra shit. Feel me?"

"You know what? Say no more. Go talk to her."

I smacked my teeth.

"How the fuck I'm supposed to do that? I don't even know where she stays."

"You got her number, right?"

I nodded.

"Aight. I got you!"

CHAPTER 18

<u>Aphrodite Samuels</u>

Bitch better have my money! Bitch better have my money! Bitch better have my, bitch better have my——.

"Aphrodite speaking. How may I help you?" I questioned with a mouth full of spaghetti, which made words came out as a bunch of mush. I had just gotten done fixing dinner for myself, and boy this shit was good. I'd made a nice pot of spaghetti with that cheesy garlic bread on the side and a tall glass of iced tea to wash it down with. Boy, I'll tell you, this was life right here. Good food and some peace... what could be better?

I heard a velvety rich laugh come from the other end of the line, causing blood to immediately rush my cheeks. *That damn Derrick*! Coughing, I quickly covered my embarrassment before responding.

"Hi, what's up?" I asked, trying to make my voice sound as clear and sultry as possible without having it sound forced. I rolled my eyes at myself and shook my head. Look at me, trying to put on the bedroom voice and shit. I needed to stop.

"Goddess?" Derrick spoke up, causing me to jump a little.

"I'm sorry. My mind is everywhere right now. But what were you saying?"

Derrick chuckled.

"Nothing really. A nigga just wanted to talk to you for a minute," he stated. I smiled at that. One thing I loved to find in a man was someone who called me just to talk. Omar always used to call me on some bullshit. He never wanted to just talk and listen to each other's voices. There was always a catch with him.

I inhaled deeply, trying to calm my emotions before slowly letting it out. Omar wasn't even worth my time right now.

"I mean, I'm eating right now, but I can talk. How was your day?" I asked coolly. I stuffed another fork full of spaghetti into my mouth as I waited for his reply.

"Good. Kareem's ass be like Anthony Davis, prone to injury."

I laughed.

"How was your day, my goddess?" he asked. I shrugged.

"Samantha and I had a best friend beach day. I met up with some friends from college. It was a very chill day today." I replied before licking a bit of spaghetti sauce from the corner of my lip. I didn't bother telling him

165

specifically who those college friends were, because one of them was Messiah. Nobody was trying to think about Messiah.

"Beach? So you're saying I could've seen you in a swimsuit? Really, Goddess? Why you ain't call me?"

"It was just a girl thing. No boys!"

I smirked, rolling my eyes as I twirled the pasta on my plate with my fork.

"Next time, I got you," I added. Derrick laughed.

"I'm gon' hold you to that——"

Knock! Knock!

The fuck, I thought, slightly confused but most of all annoyed. *Who the fuck could possibly be knocking on my door*, I mused, checking the time at the stove. It read 8:40 p.m.

"Someone's at my door, Derrick. Give me a minute," I said with a smack of my teeth before switching my phone to mute. I rolled my eyes and smacked my teeth before going to answer the door.

"Who is it?" I asked. I wasn't trying to be on *I Almost Got Away With It* or *First 48*. Shit, you couldn't trust anything these days. I'd seen *Criminal Minds*, and I was not about to be one of those women who were abducted from their home because their simple-minded ass wanted
166

to go opening doors and shit. Ain't no killer about to be standing on the other side waiting for me, like "I was waiting for you at the door."

"Get it together, Dite. Damn!" I said out loud to myself with a shake of my head before opening the door. *What the fuck?* I blinked a few times as I stared at the person in front of me. Slowly, I picked up my phone, taking it off mute before speaking.

"I'm going to have to talk to you later."

Without giving him a chance to respond, I clicked end on my phone. I sighed, where the fuck is Ashton man?

CHAPTER 19

Aphrodite Samuels

I downed back another glass of Chardonnay, yearning for it to be something stronger as I tried to fight my nerves and keep from saying something I shouldn't. I swear God must have really been playing with my life right now. I couldn't deal with this shit, man. *I just can't. I need some air,* I thought, breathing heavily

"What are you doing here, Messiah?" I asked with a slight eye roll. Messiah shrugged.

"I wanted to talk. We didn't really get a chance to talk earlier," he spoke nonchalantly as he slumped down in his seat, spreading his legs a bit. I eyed him, feeling a bit irritated as I watched him stuff some of my spaghetti into his mouth. I shook my head, over there getting comfortable and shit. Not only had this man completely barged into my house, but he also decided to fix himself a plate and get comfortable on my couch. *I must really have 'fuck with Aphrodite' written on my forehead right now. Just ridiculous.*

"Binky, what do we have to talk about?" I asked with a roll of my eyes. I stood at the breakfast bar, sipping on my Nay whilst I glared at him. *This man here.*

168

"And how do you know where I stay? Haley doesn't even know my address." I stated bluntly. There was no sense in beating around the bush. Knowing Messiah and how persistent he could be, I knew he wasn't going to leave until we "talked".

"You know I always have my ways."

I smacked my teeth.

"Nah, real talk. I missed you, best friend. I just want us to get back to where we used to be."

I gave him a look, causing him to let out a nervous chuckle.

"I mean, minus that other part. I just need your friendship. Can we be friends again?"

Should I? I mean, could we just be friends? I knew that it was hard to be friends with someone who you were in love with, but it wasn't impossible. And sure, him and Haley had done me dirty, but that was years ago. I couldn't be holding grudges anymore. I was too grown for that shit. I sighed, fixin' to say something when I heard,

"Goddess, open up the door!"

My eyes widened at the sound of Derrick's voice. What the hell was he doing here? Damn, was it pop up on Dite day? I bit my lip nervously as my eyes darted from the front door to Messiah who had a sour look on his

169

face. *The fuck was his problem*, I questioned. but I realized that it wasn't any of my concern.

"Uh, give me a sec!" I shouted back to Derrick before looking toward Messiah.

"I'm going to need you to like go to the back…" I trailed off. I mean, it's not like I was doing anything wrong, but I, sure enough, didn't want Derrick to see Messiah and think something was up. I wasn't about to miss out on what could be a good thing behind Messiah's ass.

"Really, Bam? On some side nigga shit, really?" Messiah spoke in disbelief as he shook his head at me. I scoffed.

"Whatever, man. Just go in my room," I spoke, pointing toward the hall, ignoring the ugly look he was giving me at my demand. We stared at each other for a good little minute. I was urging him to do what I said with my eyes, and he was looking at me like I had lost my mind for asking him that. A few moments later, Messiah smacked his teeth.

"I'm a grown ass man. I ain't 'bout to hide in your closet like I'm some high school ass nigga! If ol' boy got a problem, then so be it. It ain't like we were doing anything."

170

I cut my eyes at him. *This little, ugh!*

"That's not the point. He might suspect something if you're here, sitting down and eating while I'm dressed in these short ass shorts, and keep your damn voice down!" I whisper-shouted as I gestured toward my very visible thighs. Being the nigga that he was, Messiah's eyes quickly darted to my thighs. His bottom lip slipped between his teeth as he eyed them. I rolled my eyes. *The nerve.*

"Bruh, just get your ass up and go, please!" I pleaded again. Messiah's eyes traveled up until they met my own irritated and slightly vexed ones, and he smirked.

"Can we be friends again?"

I gave him a look. "What the hell, Binky? Just go, damn!"

"Not until you give me an answer."

I frowned. *This nigga.* This was some real side nigga shit, man. Ugh, he was so fucking aggravating. I'd never known him to be so damn annoying.

"Oh my God. Really?"

Messiah shrugged.

"Dead ass."

I sighed. *Fuck it, man.*

"Fine, now go!"

A smile took over Messiah's face as his greenish hazel eyes lightened at the sound of my reply.

"That's wasn't so hard, now was it?" he spoke, with a silly ass Cheshire cat grin on his face as he hopped up out of his seat. I kissed my teeth and pointed to the back again before mouthing the word go.

"Say no more!"

Big stupid smiled as he happily walked to my room.

"Got my Bambie back," I heard him say, causing me to roll my eyes at his foolishness. *Goddamn, Messiah!* Once I made sure Messiah was indeed in my room with the door shut, I quickly made my way to the front door and opened it.

"Damn, Goddess. What were you doing?" Derrick asked once he saw me. I smiled and shrugged casually.

"Nothing, so what brings you by?" I asked, trying to steady my heartbeat. I don't know why I was so nervous. I mean, maybe it was because there was a man in my room, probably in my bed, who I used to have sexual relations with, and here I was talking to the man I was, I guess, dating. This felt like some cheaters shit, swear. I mean, my loyalty lied with neither, but I still felt like I was cheating on somebody. Derrick shrugged.

172

"I just wanted to see if you were okay. You kind of ended the phone call abruptly. Didn't even let a nigga say bye."

He paused to laugh a little before continuing.

"So you're straight? Do you need a nigga to come lay-up with you and give you butt rubs until you fall asleep? 'Cause you know I'll do it."

He smirked cheekily. *Oh Lord.* I coughed and laughed. "I bet you would, but I'm okay. Everything is fine."

"So I can't come in though?"

Shit.

"I mean, uhh, I-I guess."

Really nigga?

CHAPTER 20

Aphrodite Samuels

"So, you just wasn't going to fix ya boy a plate? Really, Goddess? I thought we were better than this!" Derrick spoke, astonished as he dug into the pot of spaghetti to get the remaining pasta out of the pot. I rolled my eyes and smiled a little at his silliness as I leaned up against the kitchen island and watched him. This man was a trip.

"Boy, whatever! And I was gon' eat that later," I spoke, playfully glaring at him. Derrick gave me a 'really nigga' look as he eyed me pointedly.

"Come on, Dite. Now why you lie? You know you don't want this." he responded, gesturing toward his plate of spaghetti. I laughed.

"Okay... hurry up and get out my kitchen!"

I didn't like people in my kitchen after I had cooked. I never had. I used to tell my dad that all the time before, during, and after I cooked. I don't know why. It was just something I'd always done. Avery's ol' aggravating ass was always talking 'bout some "girl, this my kitchen. I pay the bills, but since I'm nice, I'm gon' leave you be."

"Well, damn. But I'm done. You got some garlic bread too?"

174

I watched Derrick laugh as we watched *Scream* season two, episode eight on Netflix. I eyed him, confused.

"What the hell is so funny? That dude just got shot like three times!" I uttered, honestly confused as to how amusement was found by what was taking place. Emma had just shot Eli, and now we found out that Kieran's ol' duck ass was conspiring with Piper's crazy ass. Shit, I didn't see that coming, but I knew I didn't like his ass for some reason, ol' overgrown looking ass. Boy didn't look like no damn high schooler I'd ever saw back in my day.

Dite, shut your ass up! It ain't like you was born in the 60s.

I gave a mental shrug. Whatever.

"I mean, she wanted to be mad at that black-haired broad, but her duck ass was the one giving that nigga all the fucking ammo," he replied, referring to Emma's stank ass. I ain't like her ass either, and he was right. Her dumb ass fucked that dude and let that nigga know everything that she was going to do. Like bitch, not only was he the dude new in town, but he just screamed 'I got secrets', like why the fuck would you give in to him so easily?

175

Ain't you the pot calling the kettle black? Remember, Messiah?

Goddamn Messiah. I had completely forgotten his ass was in my room. Fuck! He probably was going through my things. Lord knows when that man gets bored, he'd get nosy. I didn't have time for him to be finding something he shouldn't. I sighed. *Lord Jesus, give me the strength.*

I rolled my eyes before clicking out of the episode once I saw the end credits pop up.

"What do you want to watch next?" I asked, eyeing him from my peripheral as I browsed the horror movie section. We had decided to have a back-to-back horror marathon as we Netflix and cuddled. There was no Netflix and chilling going on tonight. Nah, I'm good.

Whatever you say, Khepri. You ain't fooling nobody, my conscience spoke up, causing me to roll my eyes at myself. *I can't, man. I try to can, but I just can't. Lord, have mercy on my soul.* I took my eyes off of the TV as I waited expectantly for Derrick's response. Derrick cleared his throat.

"I mean, what I want to watch ain't on here." he spoke, taking his eyes off of the TV screen and looking at me as he bit his lip.

176

"So what do you want to watch then?"

"You."

Wait, what?

"I wanna watch you strut across this floor wearing some long red heels in your birthday suit. Call me The Weekend because girl, I just wanna see you in your birthday suit. Take it all off. I don't wanna see you baby in those clothes..."

He began to sing, giving me those sex-you-up eyes. Blood rushed to my cheeks at the sound of his voice. He wasn't any Trey Songz, but that rich deepness of his voice made it sound like sex to the ear. I inhaled deeply.

Don't do it, Dite! We're better than this. I coughed a little to control my inner hoe's desires. I was not about to sex this man with Messiah in the other room, although I wanted to so badly. It was too early in our little relationship to be doing that anyway.

I mean, couldn't we at least see what that mouf do, though?

Sweet baby Jesus. I needed to find my chill, man. I scoffed.

"Boy, bye! You have to earn that privilege. Shit, better get it popping with Palmela when you go home because there ain't gon' be none of that tonight! I mean, either that or Pornhub."

I shrugged casually, despite the fact that I was as red as a strawberry at his previous statement. Derrick smacked his teeth and pulled me closer to him.

"I just want to love you girl," he spoke lowly in my ear as his gripped tighten around my waist.

"Can I do that, Goddess?"

Yes is what I wanted to say but I couldn't. Messiah was right in the other room, and sexing another man in my house while he was here would be so weird. I shook my head, giving off a little smirk.

"Nah, all my loving is being saved for my sheets and pillow, so what you 'bout to do?"

"Damn. Really, Goddess? Just like that?"

I shrugged.

"I mean, it is what it is."

I laughed. Like I said, there wouldn't be any Netflix and chilling. I had shit to do in the morning. Plus, big stupid was in my room, so there was that.

CHAPTER 20

<u>Aphrodite Samuels</u>

This man, here. I shook my head as I gazed at this big idiot. My ass was up here feeling like I was on an episode of cheaters, and this dude was sleeping like everything was cool and copacetic. I frowned, watching as he laid wrapped up in my brown fur throw with his head nestled in a pillow, snoring softly. *The nerve. I just can't, man.* I smacked my teeth,

"Dude, what the fuck!" I shrieked, causing Messiah to jump out of his sleep.

"This ain't what it looks like!"

I scoffed and rolled my eyes at Messiah's blunt lie and disregard for my privacy. The nerve of some people these day! What the hell made him think it was okay to hop his big ass in my bed and go to sleep? Slob was coming out his mouth and all too. *That damn Messiah!*

"Boy, what are you doing in my bed? Did I tell you that you can go to sleep? No, I don't think so!"

Messiah groaned tiredly as he shifted in my bed. He still hadn't made an attempt to get up.

"My fault. You and your little boyfriend were taking too long. Shit, a nigga was tired." he spoke nonchalantly.

"Binky, you are something else..." I trailed off, shaking my head at him. Messiah kissed his teeth before sitting up and shrugging.

"I mean, shit, you was the one out there caking and shit. Got me feeling like a side nigga or some shit."

"For you to be my side, it would require me to be in a relationship, which last time I checked, I was not. Secondly, it also requires for me to want you, but I don't."

"So you're single?"

"Really? That's all you heard. And to answer your question, I am... on a technicality. Derrick and I aren't official. We're just talking, but I like him."

I watched Messiah nod his head as he took in everything I said.

"That's legit. If you're happy, then…" he trailed off as he began to look around my room as if trying to avoid my gaze. I shook my head. He wasn't telling me something. If there was one thing I knew about Messiah, I knew that whenever he was hiding something from me, he liked to avoid eye contact. Apparently, my eyes seared into his soul, which made it hard for him to hide the truth from me.

"Really, Binky? What are you not telling me?" I asked, placing a hand on my hip as I glared at him in the

180

hopes that he'd confess his secret. Much to my disappointment, Messiah did not falter. *Bruh.* I sighed.

"Okay, don't tell me, but just so you know, friends don't keep secrets," I spoke smoothly, putting an emphasis on the word friends. Back when we were strictly friends, we never really kept secrets from each other. He was like my walking talking diary and vice versa. Either this secret must have been something really big, or maybe I was just blowing things out of proportion, and it was nothing at all. I shrugged. Whatever the case, I wasn't going to stress it.

Messiah Lafayette

"Okay, don't tell me, but just so you know, friends don't keep secrets."

Friends...

Why did that shit sound so rough coming from her? I mean, could I just be friends with Dite, or had that ship already passed? Fuck, man. I was tripping! Shrugging, I opened my mouth to reply.

"Ain't nobody hiding anything, Dite. I'm just really happy for you. You deserve it. I hope ol' dude treating you right.'"

I sighed. I couldn't even lie. A part of me didn't want to believe in the idea that she was in a relationship or even in love with another man, but she wasn't my girl, nor was she ever. I had Haley, and if ol' dude was making her happy, then so be it. I guess we'd missed our chance. Bambie frowned, eyeing me down in suspicion for a good little minute before she shrugged.

"Okay, Binky. Whatever you say," she spoke coolly, causing relief to rush through my body at the fact that she was dropping the subject. I watched her roll her eyes before walking over and sitting next to me on the bed.

"So, best friend, what's up? How's everything going with Haley and the wedding?" she asked curiously. I involuntarily smacked my teeth at the mention of Haley's name. I don't know what had been up with us lately, but for some reason, her ass had been irking my soul.

"Let's not even go there." I spoke, end this conversation before it even started.

***

"Congratulations."

"On what?" Bambie spoke, giving me a questioning look as we sat opposite each other on her bed. Its nice to just talk with somebody and with Dite its easy for a nigga to get real cerebral.

I shrugged, bringing myself out my thoughts before responding.

"On your teacher status. I knew being around little kids was always your heart."

"Oh, thanks. What do you do?"

"You know medicine was my passion. I'm a pharmaceutical rep at Johnson and Wales Pharmaceuticals."

Bambie nodded.

"That's dope. You must be bringing in that check," she joked with a slight laugh. I laughed too.

183

"Shit. I guess," I stated nonchalantly as I watched Bam sip on the wine she had brought to sip on as we talked.

"I see your ass already slurring. You were always the light weight."

I smirked. Back in college, Bambie was never the type to drink unless it was Chardonnay, and even that had her ass weak after a few sips. Bambie cut her eyes at me.

"Boy, whatever. I am good!" she slurred with a smack of her teeth.

"Yeah, whatever you say, Bam. Can I get some?"

"I mean, if you must."

Rolling her eyes, she handed me her half empty cup. I took a sip and shook my head. I didn't know how she drank that shit. Shit was too soft for me. I needed something strong. Hennessy or something. This fruity shit wasn't for me.

CHAPTER 22

<u>Messiah Lafayette</u>

Bzz! Bzz! Bzz!

"Yeah?" I spoke answering my phone that had been vibrating against my thigh for a good two minutes now.

"Really, Messiah? Where in the blue hell are you?"

Sighing, I rolled my eyes at the sound of Haley's voice. What the fuck was she on about, calling me like we were not in the same house? This broad was crazy.

Really, fam? So you just gon' forget the other night?

I groaned, blinking a few times as I looked around to adjust my eyes to the darkness. *If Haley is on the phone, then who the hell is laying on me,* I questioned, confused as fuck. *Lord, please don't tell me I don' got caught slipping.* Sighing, I slowly shifted my gaze downward. Wait a minute. Was that cherry blossom honey? I sniffed. *Damn. Dite,* I thought, realizing where the hell I was. I'd remember that smell anywhere. Damn, she smelled good. I instinctively ran my hand through her hair and was thankful to feel not one track. One thing I respected about my Dite was the fact that she didn't put any of that cheap ass horse hair in her head. All her shit was coming straight from her scalp. It was just the way I liked it, natural.

185

Shaking my head, I removed Bambie's head from my chest while slowly removing myself from out of her bed, trying to make sure that she didn't wake up.

"Are you going to answer my question, or…? You know what? All I'm gon' say is you better not be at some other bitch's house!" Haley's aggravating voice rang. I smacked my teeth. Her ass was gon' fuck around and bust a nigga's eardrum with that whining and shit.

"Whatever, Haley. Ain't nobody cheating on you," I spoke evenly, trying to keep my voice low so I wouldn't wake Dite up.

"So where are you then?"

"I'm with Trey and them. We went out for a few drinks, and everybody sleeping it off now."

I could hear Haley smack her teeth from the other side, clearly not believing me. *Bruh, I can't with this woman.*

"Whatever, Haley, man. Don't be overthinking shit. I'll be home in a lil' bit."

Without giving her a chance to respond, I hung up the phone on her ass. I shook my head. *Fucking Haley.*

"Tell Haley I said hey," I heard as I slipped on my sneakers. I smacked my teeth. I didn't know if Bambie was trying to be funny or not, but she didn't make me feel

186

any better with that statement. I was not trying to hear Haley's high-pitched ass voice go on and on about me possibly cheating on her or some shit when I got home.

"Whatever, Bambie. Since you're awake, come walk me out."

Bambie groaned at my request, shifting her body so that her back was now to me.

"Boy, bye!"

I sucked in a breath, ignoring what she had said. *That ass, though.* She was sleeping in a tank top with those short, shorts from the night before that gave me all types of views of that ass. The shit was sitting all plump and shit, just calling out to me.

Better grab that shit and move that thing like handlebar! Give in, my nigga. We all know you want to.

I ain't about to do that shit! I got a girl, and she's seeing someone. Ugh, fuck my life, man!

I heard Bambie laugh lazily, bringing me out of my thoughts.

"Better go, before she revokes your meal privileges. You know Haley don't play."

I cut my eyes at her.

"Oh, you got jokes now? Okay."

Without even thinking, I laid a firm, hard slap on her right ass cheek before taking off.

"MESSIAH!"

***

"So you just gon' sit up here in my face and lie?"

I mugged her.

"Man, watch out. I already don' told your insecure ass I wasn't cheating on you!" I spoke, sidestepping her and making my way to our room.

"But you ain't tell me the truth, though! I know your ass wasn't with no damn Trey. I tracked your phone to an unknown location. Your ass lucky I ain't pull up and drop that bitch you were with!" Haley's ol' aggravating ass snapped as she trailed after me.

Wait a minute. I stopped mid-stride. I knew damn well this woman ain't say she had tracked my motherfucking phone. The fuck kind of shit was she on? *Bruh.* I turned to look at her.

"Are you stupid or just plain crazy? The fuck? You tracking me and shit?" I fumed, clearly vexed. For her to say she had been tracking me, she was basically telling me that she didn't trust my ass, and one thing my mama told me was that if a female didn't trust you, then she didn't love you. I wasn't trying to be involved with a

188

broad who didn't respect, appreciate, and trust me to love and take care of her. I sighed.

"You know what? I ain't got time for your shit right now. I'm tired, and you tripping. So what I'm about to do is go to sleep and let you be."

I shook my head at her before turning to leave. I was done for the night.

CHAPTER 23

Two weeks later

<u>Aphrodite Samuels</u>

"Boy, bye! We all know what you want. You ain't slick!" I spoke with a smack of my teeth as I twirled a strand of my hair while I conversed with Derrick on my lunch break. I had a good fifteen minutes to spare before I had to go get my kids when Derrick had hit me up. Apparently, he wanted to see me later on tonight, but we all know how that goes. He just wanted that booty!

Girl, if you don't get your mans! I'm 'bout tired of your shit.

I rolled my eyes at my inner conscience, or should I say my inner hoe as she tried to coax me into giving in to my inner desires. Although Derrick and I had been talking for a good little minute, we were still taking things slow, real slow. I felt that good things came to those who waited, and if he wanted this good thing, then he'd wait. I laughed. Let me stop. I was over her acting like I was all that and a box of Krispy Kreme doughnuts.

"Now why I always gotta want something from you? Maybe I just want to spend time with my woman. Is that so hard to believe?" Derrick asked, seemingly appalled at my accusations. *This man here.* I mused with a shake of

190

my head. He was truly something else. *I can't with him*. I scoffed.

"Derrick, we all know what you're trying to do with me, but it ain't gon' be no baby making tonight!"

"See, I ain't even trying to get you pregnant. Just let me swim in your ocean for a bi-"

"Dude! I am at work. Have you no shame?" I questioned, slightly blushing at his unfinished statement. I swear this man was something else. He knew damn well I was at work. I couldn't be feeling all hot and bothered right now. I had twenty kids to worry about. I shook my head. *No shame*.

Derrick laughed.

"You know I wouldn't be me if I didn't get a lil` nasty. Nah, I'm just playing, Goddess. I know that ain't for you, and I'm willing to take it as slow as you want. I mean, as long as you're feeling me and vice versa, we're good," he spoke sincerely, causing my heart to beat faster. *Music to my ears. Lord Jesus, this man better know what he's doing to me!*

"I-I-I ugh... I mean, that's good to hear. Listen, I'm gon' have to get at you later. Stop by my house tonight."

With that being said, I hung up the phone before shaking my head. *That damn Derrick.*

191

God must be really testing me. Currently, I was sitting with Haley, Mariah wannabe Carey, Niamey, and Asia going over some shit for Haley's wedding. Haley wanted us to come to a cake tasting with her and her man who had yet to show up to this little shindig.

This bitch was on some other shit this evening. Her ass wasn't even allowing us to eat anything until her man got here. To be honest, I wanted to punch her ass in the face. My ass could've been watching *Prison Break* until Derrick arrived while I stuffed my face with Doritos, but no. My dumb ass decided to grace Haley and her posse with my presence.

I swear, if Messiah didn't get his ass on somewhere, we were gon' have to fight. There were three things I didn't play about; my food, my sleep, and my job. I sighed. *You know what? Let me text this fool.* While all the girls were talking, I whipped out my phone, went into my messages, and went to the thread titled "Bitch ass Messiah."

Me: Bring that ass Binky!

Messiah: Dite??

I rolled my eyes. Like, who else would it be? He knew damn well I was the only one that called him that.

192

Me: Yeah, your woman won't let us eat if you're not here, so I'm going to need you to hurry up.

I was already done with the conversation. See, I was what you'd call a "hangry" person. I'd get angry when I was hungry, and right now, my belly was itching for some food. Being the good ass "friend" that I was, I was trying to support my "friend", but this bitch was trying it, and I was not having it today. Haley and Messiah were gon' fuck around get their asses fucked up, fucking around with my patience.

Messiah: My fault, Dite. I'm with Trey right now.

Boy, don't anybody care, I thought with a shake of my head and click of my teeth. My stomach was on E. All I wanted to do was get fed. After work, I didn't have time to stop and put something on my stomach, because Haley's ass wanted to constantly blow up my phone on some reckless shit. If I didn't get any food soon, it was gon' be like World War Z up in here. I sighed. I wasn't even about to respond to his ass. I quickly clicked out of my messenger before deciding to play a game on my phone.

"Who are you texting?"

My eyes immediately went up, catching Haley's gaze. *This bitch*! Shrugging, I simply told her nobody and tuned back to the conversation with everybody else.

***

"So, Aphrodisiac, how do you feel about being Haley's maid of honor?"

Bitch, I cut my eyes at Thing 2 AKA Mariah no Carey before looking back down at my phone. It had been a good fifteen minutes since I had texted Messiah, and while the other girls talked and shit, I was over here playing Choices, an interactive story game. Laughing, I rolled my eyes. This bitch thought she was big and bad. When I dropped her ass on her neck, she was gon' think I'd done her wrong, ol' petty ass.

/"I'm pretty sure my daddy named me Aphrodite, but since you wanna be ignorant, I'm gon' tell you straight up. I don't like your ass. The reason why I haven't rocked your shit is because I'm a grown ass woman! I don't have time to fight or argue with your wannabe Barbie ass. Haley already knows Avery mothafucking Samuels ain't raise a punk, so this is your warning. Cross me again, and I'm gon' show you one," I spoke calmly, without looking up from my phone. Your girl was hungry, and my patience was really running low.

194

"Matter of fact," I spoke as I was fixin' to get up and leave. Just as I was getting up, in walked Messiah's ass looking like he had just come from a funeral.

CHAPTER 24

Messiah Lafayette

"If it isn't the man of the hour! Mr. Lafayette. I'm glad you could make it."

I nodded at some Caucasian man who greeted me with a bright ass Cheshire cat grin. Dude looked a little fruity. but that was none of my business. To be honest. I wasn't even stuntin' anybody else but Bambie. It was crazy, but it was the truth. Her ass looked hella good today. That little tank top shit she had on brought her titties to my attention, front and center. And that purple, boy, she knew she always looked good in purple. Them lips looked like two big velvety purple pillows. *Damn, can I just suck on 'em one last time?*

I subconsciously licked my lips at the thought.

"My fault. Lost track of time," I spoke, snapping back into reality as I looked from Bambie to Haley. My eyes lingered on Bambie a bit more than they should have, and I could clearly see the agitation written all over her face. I mentally laughed. *Same old Dite*. I knew her ass was starving by the way she mugged everybody, especially Haley, and if I knew Dite, I knew she wasn't having it. We'd probably have to call twelve in a minute. She was looking like she was ready to jump across the floor, and

196

Molly whop Haley's ass. Her ass didn't play about her food. She was a force to be reckoned with when she got hungry. I sighed. *Man, I love that girl.*

Aphrodite Samuels

Why the fuck does he keep staring at me like that? I rolled my eyes as my stomach growled.

"Well look who decided to show his ass! So Haley, baby girl, can we eat now?" I asked with a smack of my teeth as I eyed Haley in annoyance. I swear, I was like two seconds away from pouncing on this heifer, on some real shit. Her ass had all of us up in here starving, all because her man wasn't here. I mean, I doubt he cared what cake was gon' be at this uppity ass wedding anyway.

"I mean, don't you think you should skip a few meals. You could afford to lose a few pounds."

Wait a minute. I know damn well... Did sh—this bitch! I laughed a humorless laugh as I eyed Mariah's old stinking ass.

"I see you. Lil' mama thinks she's cute. That's cool."

With that being said, I rose up out of my seat with my half-empty glass of champagne in hand. I smiled, taking a sip of my drink before nodding. Man, fuck this shit. With that in mind, I threw the rest of the champagne at her and popped that hoe straight in the mouth.

"Dit—"

198

"Nah, Haley. Don't Dite me. She's your friend, so you should've told her to stop trying me. I ain't the one!" I snapped with a roll of my eyes at Haley's confidence. I hope she didn't think she was going to check me. Ol' girl deserved it. *Fuck she mean?* I scoffed

"You know what? Ain't nobody got time for the shit. I'm out!"

***

"Not the drink Goddess! Tell me you ain't waste that expensive ass champagne on that broad?"

I shrugged, running my hands up and down Derrick's bare chest as he stared up at me in astonishment. I sat, straddling him on my bed as we talked about what had happened earlier at Haley's cake tasting event.

"I mean, she kept fucking with me. I had to put that hoe in her place," I stated nonchalantly as I licked my lips at the sight of his perfectly toned chest. It was all smooth and shit, just the way I liked it.

Derrick chuckled.

"I guess I got a mini gangster on my hands."

He paused, smirking.

199

"I like that!" he finished, rubbing his hands up my thighs. I grabbed them, stopping him from reaching my butt.

"Don't try it!"

"Dite, you know that ass is calling a nigga. I can't help it."

I kissed my teeth. This dude was so corny. "My ass is not up for grabs... literally."

Derrick nodded.

"Bet."

With that being said, he quickly flipped us over. My back collided with the gray sheets on the bed, causing my heart to jump a little. I didn't know what was going on in his mind at the moment, but I knew him well enough to know that he could get really nasty if he wanted to. I honestly didn't know if I was ready for all that. I mean, I wanted to, but I was still hesitant.

"What's on your mind? Why you frowning?" Derrick broke out, bringing me out of my thoughts. His warm brown eyes held a look of concern and worry in them, causing me to sigh. Here I was, wasting time being afraid to take the next step with this heaven-sent man all over some shit that had happened years ago. Lord, what was wrong with me? I huffed.

200

"Truth be told, I'm afraid."

"Afraid of what?"

"This… us… you. I mean, it's not you. It's definitely me. To be honest, I've only been in a serious relationship twice in my whole entire life. Both times, I gave my all and got that shit thrown back into my face. I just can't go through that shit again. You know?"

Derrick hummed in response to my lil' confession. He nodded.

"I feel you, but like a wise man once said. You win some. You lose some, but you live. You live to fight another day! Nah, for real though. As long as I got you and you got me, forget that shit that your exes did. I ain't them, and I promise that if you let me, I'll show... a different stroke."

He smirked, grinding himself up on me.

"Derrick!" I hissed and then moaned in shock. Why was he so big? *God, my ovaries.*

Damn.

"Uhh… Derrick, I can—"

"Ssh... I got this. Let me do me and do you," he spoke coolly as he began to trail his lips along my exposed flesh on my neck. His hands found their way to hem of my black Nike running shorts.

201

"You know I won't give you this D today, but I would like a taste of my goddess. Can I do that?"

Without giving me a chance to reply, he swiftly removed my shorts. Before he began to play with my clit, his long, slender finger entered me, giving me no time for preparation. I moaned again, trying to keep it on the low. I was not trying to have my neighbors hear my moans through these walls tonight. That was just embarrassing. One finger came to two as he went in and out inside of me really fast. He soon replaced his fingers with his tongue, and it was all over from then. He started sucking on my clit again, making his tongue go all types of ways. I grabbed on to his head, pushing his face deeper, wanting more.

"U-ugh." I sighed, eyes practically rolling to the back of my head. *I just can't.* My breathing began to pick up its tempo as I felt my release coming. He stopped eating me and rubbed my clit, pinching it. He looked up to me, watching how I reacted. I looked up, closing my eyes and enjoying the pleasure.

"Mmmmmm."

"Cum for me, Goddess," he said in a deep husky voice. He went back to eating me, and I was so close.

202

With a flick of his tongue, I came hard, moaning his name.

"Mmmm, Derrick."

He kept on fingering me, sending another wave of that good feeling through my body. My juices went flowing, and he licked my thigh up to my pussy, not missing a single drop. He sat back up.

"Damn, you really do taste like peaches!"

CHAPTER 25

<u>Aphrodite Samuels</u>

BANG! BANG!

Fuck. I silently cursed at the sound of someone making a beat at my door. I sighed. *Black people these days.* I mused with a shake of my head before rolling over in my bed. I was going to try my best to ignore the constant banging at my door because all I wanted to do was sleep. I was just too damn tired to get up at the moment. I swear, I don't know how tired work had me until the weekend officially hit.

BANG! BANG!

"Girl, open the door. This yo' daddy!" I heard. Immediately, I perked up. *What the hell is he doing here, and why the fuck is he so loud.* I questioned myself anxiously and a bit irritated. I really didn't feel like getting my ass beat, especially on a Saturday. *God, please let this be a check-up visit and not a whoop that ass visit.* I silently prayed before dragging myself out of bed. I mean, my dad visited me here and there, but that was rare. He stayed in Savannah, and he didn't like driving long distances.

I quickly slipped on a pair of navy blue Adidas gym shorts over my pink boy shorts before I grudgingly made my way out of my room and down the hall into the living room to unlock the door.

"Khepri! Girl, you better open this do— That's what I thought!"

I slightly rolled my eyes as I stared at the big, swole six-foot-four tatted dark caramel brown-skinned man before me.

"Daddy!" I sang, opening my arms for a hug. He stale faced me before using his right hand to push me out of the way. *Well damn.* I thought, shaking my head at the audacity of Avery Samuels. Well shit. I thought we were cool.

That's what I get for thinking.

"What you got to eat in here? I'm starving! Been stuck in the damn car for 'bout three hours, and yo' daddy hungry and tired. My bag is in the car. If you can go get them for me, that'll be nice."

The fuck.

"After that, can you fix your old man something to eat?" he added, causing me to side eye him as I shut the door. *The nerve of some people.* I mused, shaking my head. *Man, I can't with people these days. Avery a trip.* I rolled my eyes.

"Nice to see you too, Avery," I spoke sarcastically as I walked over to him. My dad mugged me before smacking his teeth. His attitude, man...

"Girl, don't be putting my government out there like that! You know I got warrants."

I blinked. *That damn Avery*, I thought with a small chuckle. I swear, my daddy was a mess, man.

"Whatever, old man. You're lucky I'm nice."

"And you're lucky I ain't trying to catch a case. Girl, you know I'll box your ass. Don't play!"

He mugged me before taking a seat on my sofa and switching on the TV. I shook my head at his foolishness, deciding not to say anything before heading into the kitchen to start cooking.

I decided to make something simple, so I took out some steak and placed it in the sink before running some hot water over it. I knew my dad preferred his steak with potatoes, which was why I decided to pair the steak with smashed roasted garlic and herb potatoes. I pulled out a large pot from one of the bottom cupboards to start boiling the water for my potatoes. Once the water started to boil, I placed the potatoes inside. Next, I gathered the rest of the ingredients for the food and went to work on our meal.

***

I smiled slightly, looking down at my masterpiece of a meal as my dad was cackling in the other room due to whatever he was watching. I sighed. *I hope once he eats, he won't be so quick to beat my ass if that's the case*, I mused, wincing a little at the thought of my twenty-five-year-old ass getting an ass whooping like I was ten again. Hopefully, he'd be full and wanting to take a nap, one of those long three-day coma type naps.

Shrugging, I pulled myself out of my thoughts before calling my dad into the kitchen.

"See, this is what I missed, you making your old man a good meal occasionally. You already know I ain't with that cooking shit," he spoke, rubbing his hands together greedily as he eyed his very full plate of steak, green beans, and potatoes. He'd probably only come down here for the food. His old ass didn't miss me. He missed my cooking. I rolled my eyes. *Just fake*.

"You are something else, Avery."

I shook my head at him before grabbing my plate and making my way out of the kitchen.

"I ain't trying to have no roaches, so can you please eat your food in the dining room?" I called over my shoulder. My dad was a messy eater who liked eating in front of the TV, and I personally was not a big fan of finding bones and shit in my sofa. I heard him smack his teeth before responding.

"Girl, who do you think you are, acting like you and them roaches didn't use to play Monopoly and shit when you were growing up? Girl, I caught you play fighting with their asses, and now you have the audacity to be bougie. Shit, you and the roaches were raised in the same house, but since I'm nice, I'm gon' let it slide," he replied with a slight laugh. *Ain't nothing funny*, I thought but refrained from retaliating. I simply placed my plate on the table and sat down. My dad followed suit and began to demolish his plate, leaving me to sit there just waiting.

Personally, I was too scared to eat. I didn't know why my dad was here, and I was honestly afraid to ask. After a moment or two of agonizing silence, he finally spoke up.

"Who has two thumbs and has been invited to Jiminy Cricket and Michael Ealy's wedding?"

"Daddy, please tell me you said no," I whined, silently praying that he did not agree to be a part of this madness. I mean, it was one thing for me to be a part of some bullshit like this, but it was another for Avery to be involved in this shit. Avery didn't like Haley because of her new personality, and he'd made that clear to me and

208

her ass, so if he agreed to come to this child's wedding, something had to be up his sleeve. I sighed.

"What are you doing, Samuels?" I asked with a slight shake of my head at my dad's sly grin. He was definitely up to something. He shrugged.

"Girl, bye! I'm doing my civic duty of the year. That's all. This is charity," he spoke nonchalantly. I cut my eyes at him. *This man here. Charity my ass.*

"Yeah, okay, Avery..." I trailed off sarcastically with a roll of my eyes.

"Whatever, girl. I'm yo' daddy. You ain't got to believe me. Just don't question me again, and that's all I'm gon' say."

CHAPTER 26

Aphrodite Samuels

"Can anyone tell me what the people who write stories are called?"

I paused and proceeded to scan the group to see which child had their hand up. I noticed Jamie did, so I called on him. I watched a smile take over his small face before responding.

"An illustrator!" he spoke excitedly, causing me to laugh and shake my head.

"Not quite. Good answer though. Ayura, can you help Jaime out?" I said, giving my attention to a new kid named Ayura. Like Emma, he was a quiet child, so I made it my mission to try to incorporate them in circle time as much as possible, that way he could get used to group talking and be more comfortable sharing with others.

"They're called authors," Ayura replied lowly. I nodded my head in approval with a small smile on my face at his answer.

"Exactly! Authors are the people who write the words in the books we read alongside the illustrators who..." I trailed off while pointing at Diamond to finish my sentence.

210

"Draws the pictures!" she responded, matching Jamie's previous excitement.

"Right. Authors write the story, and the illustrators draw the pictures, but sometimes, the author and illustrator are the same people."

I stopped to pick up the green book that sat at my right before showing it to everyone.

"This book, *Are You My Mother?* By P. D. Eastman, is a prime example of how an author can also be an illustrator and vice versa."

I then began to ask the children questions about the book's cover and title in order to form an assumption of what the book would be about before actually reading it.

***

"Girlfriend, can you take me home?"

"Aroo?"

Jamie laughed nervously as I eyed him weirdly. Now, he was claiming me at work.

He was 'bout to make me catch a case behind his little self. I shook my head. This child was something else.

"Alright now, Mr. Carter. Where is your mama anyway?" I asked him as I began to wipe the bleach and water mixture off of the tables. It was now 3:30, and everyone from my class had gone home except Jamie. Usually, he was like the first one to leave when the day was over with. Jamie shrugged.

"I don't know," he answered nonchalantly as he skimmed through the book he was reading over in the library area. I sighed.

"Let's just see if Mommy comes in the next five minutes. If not, I'll see what I can do," I said sympathetically. I knew he was bored out of his mind over there by himself, and I had to clean up this class, so I couldn't entertain him. Jamie nodded.

"Okay, girlfri—I mean, Ms. Sam," Jamie replied, giving me a Puss In Boots look at his almost slip up. I shook my head. Lord Jesus, give me the strength.

Messiah Lafayette

"What do you mean you need me to pick up Jamie?"

"Nigga, what the hell do you think I mean? Shawn and I are a little busy, so can you like do your favorite cousin a favor?"

Favorite cousin? Nigga, you're my only cousin; I thought mentally, shaking my head at my cousin, Dante.

"What you mean y'all busy? That's y'all so— mmm, y'all nasty!"

I laughed. These niggas had a damn six-year-old, and they were over here thinking about freaking. I mean, shit. I got it, but damn. A nigga had shit to do!

No the hell you don't. Plus, you know Bambie is his teacher.

Damn, Bambie. I thought, subconsciously licking my bottom lip. Ever since ol' girl stormed out of that lil' cake tasting shit the other day, a nigga had been feeling some type of way. I didn't want to see her leave, but that ass in those jeans made me love to see her go.

Again, nigga, you have a girl!

Man, don't even get me started on Haley's ass. After her crazy ass told me she was tracking me, I damn near lost my patience with her ass. If her ass loved me, then

213

she should trust me. I knew me and Bambie had a little something back then, but that shit was old news. All I wanted and needed was her friendship now.

Plus a benefit or two.

I mentally shook my head at myself. I had to stop thinking like that. Bambie and I were just friends, but like any man, I knew an attractive female when I saw one. I mean, my Bambie was fine, and there was nothing else to it.

"Aight, man. Damn!"

With that being said, I quickly ended the call. I shook my head. *Damn, Dante!* Sighing, I ran a hand across my face in frustration. A nigga couldn't catch a break! Sometimes a nigga just wanted to do him, but now I had to do this shit. Man, fuck!

I kissed my teeth and shook my head and shrugged. *Might as well call Dite's ass. Ain't trying to be on no surprise type shit.* With that, I whipped out my phone and dialed star seventy-five because I had her ass on speed dial. It rang about ten times before Dite's sultry, raspy voice responded.

"Aphrodite Samuels speaking. How may I help you?"

Her white ass reply came through, causing me to shake my head at the fact that she was still answering the phone like that 'til this day. I chuckled.

"Ol' white ass!"

"Binky?"

I kissed my teeth. "Didn't I tell you about that damn nickname? Put some respek on my name and I ain't gon' say it no more!" I mimicked Birdman.

The way her breathing switched up on the phone, I could tell she was catching an attitude. Damn, I loved her ass.

Don't even get in your feelings, my nigga. Gon' just stop you right there.

I shook my head. Dite had a nigga going crazy. I needed to go to a mental institution, swear. I could hear Dite's soft laughter come from the other end.

"But you ain't say that to Weezy and them. For real, why are you calling me?" she asked in a no bullshit tone. *Well damn. Ain't even trying to have a conversation with a nigga.*

I smacked my teeth. "I just wanted to let you know I'm on my way to pick up Jamie. His people on some other shit at the moment."

"Just nasty, but whatever. Better hurry up. This boy is getting agitated, and as much as I love him, this is my time to give him back to his real family. I got to go!"

This woman.

"That's legit, Bambie. I got you though. Why you in a rush?" I questioned. Her ass was probably going out with that Samuel nigga. She was trying to toss my lil' cousin away over some dick that probably wasn't all that good anyway. Man, fuck that shit. Dite was a mess.

Bambie clicked her tongue.

"You don't need to know my businesses. Worry about your own self."

But you are my business was what I wanted to say, but I refrained. She really wasn't my business anymore. I mean, she was just my friend. That's all a nigga needed. Who cares if she was going out with ol' dude. At least he was treating her right. I had nothing but love for that.

So you say.

"Cool. I'll see you when I see you, B."

CHAPTER 27

Aphrodite Samuels

"Cool. I'll see you when I see you, B." I heard Messiah say before hanging up on the other end of the call. I shook my head, feeling like AJ from *The Fairly Odd Parents*. I mean, I guess people just didn't say goodbye anymore. Whatever. With a slight eye roll, I plastered a big megawatt smile on my face before addressing the small and slightly unsettled child who simply clicked around on the website Star Fall as he sat in front of one of the four computers in our class.

"Good news, Jamie. You'll be going home really soon. Your cousin, Messiah, will be here any minute now to get you," I spoke, low key grinning at the idea of finally being able to go home to my man AKA my bed. Like I said, I loved all my children when it came to my classroom, but once 3:30 hit, I was gladly ready to give them back to their parents. I couldn't wait to lay on my new 100% black silk bedding. That shit was worth every single dime and penny. It was so damn comfortable! It had my ass feeling like I was royalty or something. Ugh! Just thinking about my bed had me feeling all warm and things. Man, I missed my bed!

217

I shook my head to clear my thoughts and tuned back into reality.

"Girlfriend, how do you know Sy Sy?"

Lord Jesus, this child here, I mused with a slight chuckle. *I can't with these children of today.* Here I thought my lil' Jamie was all shy and things, but ever since his birthday, he had been slick calling me his "girlfriend". I mean, it was cute up until a certain point, but we were at my place of business for crying out loud! I could catch a case behind that little boy and his mouth. Thank the Lord everybody knew my character and understood that "lifestyle" wasn't for me. I kissed my teeth.

"Don't even go there with me, Mr. Carter. And to answer your question, me and your cousin go way back. He's actually marrying a friend of mine."

I paused, noticing how ugly the word friend sounded in regard to Haley. Damn, we really hadn't been vibing anymore. I remembered when her ass used to be my road dog. Now she was just Haley. *It is what it is.*

"Any who, why do you ask?" I questioned. I watched Jamie's little shoulders go up and down.

"He be talking about you, Ms. Sam," he spoke, causing me to frown. Part of me wanted to know what he

218

was saying about me, but another part was like fuck it. *It is what it is.* I hummed, deciding not to respond and just wait for ol' dumb ass to arrive.

***

"Jamie, that's not how you play UNO."

"Yes it is!"

"Who told you that?"

"My mama."

What in the world, I thought, staring at Jamie in amazement at the fact that he thought he could place a card down after using a wild card in the game UNO. This kid was serious with it too. He even thought that he could continue to place cards down back to back as if he kept skipping my turn which made it easy for him to win the game. Apparently, I was the one who didn't know how to play right, and I was just mad because he kept winning. We were on our third round of UNO, and Messiah had yet to arrive. This little boy had been cheating this whole entire time and wouldn't listen to me explain how to play the game.

"I know Mrs. Carter didn't teach you th—"

"Yo, sorry I'm late," I heard someone say, causing my head to snap in the direction of the voice. *Bruh, fucking*

Messiah. Shrugging. I sighed whilst pulling myself from off of the circle time rug in order to greet Messiah.

"It's fine. Jamie's things are already packed, and he's ready to go. Also, be sure to have his parents sign his daily folder report and place it back in his bag so that I can get it in the morning," I stated professionally. Messiah snickered a little, giving me that infamous Messiah smirk.

"Why so professional, Bambie? You act like you don't know a brotha," he teased.

"Can I get a hug?" he added, causing me to scoff. *Jesus, please take the wheel.*

"Binky, don't even start. I'm already tired, so you and lil' man over there need to go on 'bout y'all's business so I can go home to my man."

I laughed at the fact that I was still referring to my bed as my man. I swear, I was legit crazy.

"Mmm. Your man? You mean that lil' Samuel nigga?" Messiah spoke up, seemingly agitated. The fuck was his problem, and who the hell was Samuel?

"Samuel?" I questioned, confused as to who the fuck this Samuel guy was that I apparently was with. Messiah smacked his teeth, clearly vexed for whatever reason.

220

"Don't play, Aphrodite. You know I'm talking about that lil' nigga you were with at the beach way back when."

Wait a minute. Is this fool talking about Sam?

"Sam?"

"Yeah, that nigga."

I laughed.

"Well, that nigga is a female whose name is actually Samantha, not Samuel, who also happens to be my best friend."

I smiled at the fact that he thought Sam was my so called my man. This dude was a trip, and I knew damn well he wasn't getting all worked up over "Sam." Messiah grinned sheepishly.

"Well shit, my bad. Ugh! Let's go, Jamie!" he called out to Jamie who was busy straightening up the deck of UNO cards.

"Don't be embarrassed, Messiah. It was an honest mistake."

I shrugged, trying to ease his embarrassment. I mean, it really was. Sam was a guy's name also, so I'd understand why he thought those dots connected.

"Mmm hmm."

Messiah went with a shrug without really looking me in the eyes as he looked to Jamie who was slipping on his backpack.

"I'll talk to you later, Dite." Messiah spoke coolly before leaving with Jamie. *Ugh! God, you be having some fun with my life, don't you?*

CHAPTER 28

Messiah Lafayette

"So like can we get Mickey's or no?"

I smacked my teeth and looked back at Jay using the rear-view mirror. I noticed the lil' nigga was tapping away on that big ass iPad his extra ass mama had gotten him for his birthday. *A goddamn shame.* I thought. I still couldn't believe she spent damn near $1000 on some damn tablet for a fucking six-year-old. All a nigga got for his sixth birthday was a cupcake, one candle, and some motherfucking books.

I mean, the books were straight, but my mama wouldn't dare spend fucking $1000 dollars on one motherfucking gift for my lil' ass. She'd hit me with that "best to get it cracking with them books, lil' boy. Reading is fundamental, emphasis on the fun. Gon' and play somewhere now!" I mean, growing up, that shit was mad annoying, but once I got my first job, I realized that shit was expensive, so I had to be smart with a young nigga's money. I wasn't trying to be broke like all my homies. Nah, that wasn't for me. I had to become Julius from *Everybody Hates Chris* with my money.

"Sy Sy!"

"Nigga, what? Damn!" I snapped back at Jay. This lil'
nigga was gon' get a nice lil' whooping if he kept yelling
in my ear and shit. I could hear the lil' attitude in
his voice.

"We going to Mickey's or nah?"

Alright now. If his ass kept it up, I was gon' give his
ass an old-fashioned whooping. I coughed.

"You got some McDonald money? Is your mama gon'
pay me? Is Dante gon' pay me? If the answer to any one
of these questions is no, then I'm sorry, but it's a no for
me," I spoke with a shrug. He wasn't my son, and we
were almost to his house anyway. Why the fuck would I
waste money when I'd already burned damn near twenty
dollars' worth of gas coming down here to pick his ass
up. I knew for a fact this kid could eat, so I wasn't trying
to fuck around and drop a couple bands on his ass over
some damn McDonalds. He'd better get it popping with
that bologna and shit. His mama stayed having that fridge
packed, so it wasn't like he didn't have food at home. And
I knew a nigga had the means to get a nigga a happy meal
or two, but I was frugal than a mothafucker!

Jay kissed his teeth but didn't say anything. He
already knew the business. Nobody had time for no damn
hissy fit. To be honest, I was low-key embarrassed. I

couldn't believe I damn near went off on Bambie behind some chick named Samantha. I didn't even know why I was mad. She could do what the fuck she wanted to do, and I couldn't say shit about it. We were just friends, so it was whatever, really.

Lie again, my dude.

Man, I sighed. I knew I wasn't still pining after Dite's ass. We were way past those college days, and we were grown now. I had my thing, and she had hers. I shouldn't have even cared if she fucked with some nigga named Samuel, or any nigga for that matter. I was tripping. I shook my head. The fuck was wrong with me?

***

"So you went to go see Dite?"

Bruh, a nigga can't piss in peace! I mugged the fuck out of Haley from my peripheral as she gave me that signature stank ass look she seemed to always have lately. The fuck was wrong with this female, straight up, all on a nigga in the bathroom. And who the fuck told her about that shit? You know what, her ass probably was following a nigga on some stalker shit. Like on my soul, she was about to get her feelings hurt behind her insecurities.

"So you ain't gon' say shit? You really got me fucked up, Messiah! I ain't the one to be played, so if you and

225

Dite think y'all gon' fuck around with each other, then you got another thing coming. I'll light that ass on fire!"

Haley fumed, causing me to shake my head at her overly dramatic ass, talking 'bout some light that ass on fire. If this girl didn't go on somewhere with that mess. She knew I was no punk ass nigga, and we both knew Dite would lay the ass out in a heartbeat if she had to. My Dite could throw them hands if she needed to. I mean, Haley may have been crazy, but Dite had that calm crazy essence about her. You wouldn't want to fuck with her, and judging by her lil' incident with that broad Mariah, she hadn't changed her ways. I sighed.

"Man. I ain't trying to hear your shit. All I was doing was picking up my cousin. You know she's his teacher." I spoke tiredly as I zipped up my pants before flushing the toilet and bypassing her. I was just gon' take a good ass nap. Nobody was trying to get into it with her ass today.

"Wait." I heard Haley say before latching herself onto my arm. I kissed my teeth.

"What, B?" I asked, groaning. Why the fuck wouldn't she leave me alone?

"Well, you ain't got to be nasty. I just wanted to say I was sorry for my jealousy. You know you and Dite have history, and I just get caught up in that. You know I love you, right?"

"Mmm hmm."

"Don't do that. I'm serious," Haley spoke sincerely, looking up at me with a pout on her face. I shook my head and sighed.

"I know, and I love you too."

With that said, I leaned down and kissed her before walking off. Haley followed, and I already knew what she was trying to get into.

CHAPTER 29

<u>Aphrodite Samuels</u>

"Right in between lust and love, you go and mess things up, but now there's no we, babe. There's just you and there's me, babe."

I sang along with my girl Jennifer Hudson to "Think Like A Man" as I massaged the OGX argan oil conditioner into my scalp whilst the hot water from the shower cascaded down my body. Lord, I tell you, there was nothing better than a good relaxing shower after a long day of teaching a class of five and six-year-olds. The hot water just had a way of easing my worries or frustrations that may have developed throughout the day. See, I didn't even need to spend all that money at a damn spa. One hour in a hot steamy shower along with some good quality music was just fine for me.

"Now I'm gonna keep it realer with you now than I've ever been. We should have never been. Girl, we was better friends," Ne-Yo's part went, causing me to slightly twist my lips up in distaste before rolling my eyes and sighing at the thought of Messiah. *I'm not even trying to get into that right now,* I mused with a shake of my head. I was just trying to get clean and ease my mind so that I could sleep peacefully tonight. *Lemme gon' ahead and change this song,* I thought, opening my mouth to speak.

"Hey, Alexa. Play Khelani."

"Crazy"

I go, I go, I go, I go

Everything I do, I do it with a passion

If I gotta be a bitch, I'mma be a bad one

I bobbed my head to Khelani's voice and proceeded to
scrub my body with my loofah as the thought of Messiah
gradually left my mind.

***

BANG! BANG! BANG! BANG!

*Man, what the fuck? You know what? I'm just going to let
Avery's ass answer that. Lord knows it is too early for this
foolishness. And why the fuck are they knocking so loud? Gon'
wake up the whole neighborhood with that mess. Lord Jesus,
give me the strength.*

Evil Kermit like thoughts swirled inside my mind at the
sound of the seemingly never-ending knocking coming from
the front of my apartment. Oh the things I wanted to do to the
person on the other side of that damn door! I mean, shit. If at
first you don't succeed, try and try again, but now wasn't the
time for perseverance. Didn't they know people had shit to do
in the mornings? I had to get my sleep!

BANG! BANG!

Oh, my damn, I thought, feeling like Tommy from *Martin*.

"Khepri, girl, get the damn door!" my dad shouted from
my room. Apparently, he liked silk, and my bed makes him
feel like a king should feel. I swear, his old ass was a trip…

229

just gon' kick me out of my room like that and didn't ask or anything. Talking 'bout *you took my youth, so I'm gon' take your room,* making it seem like I was the one to give him all those gray hairs and not father time. Ugh! I couldn't with his ass sometimes. He had me out here sleeping on this uncomfortable ass sofa.

I growled lowly, pulling myself up off the couch. *Fuck, my back!* I winced, reaching up to stretch a little. I shuddered at the loud popping sound of my back cracking before shaking my head to try to perk myself up. *This better be good,* I thought before grudgingly making my way to the door.

"Who is it?"

"Messiah!"

"Go away!" I shouted back with a roll of my eyes. I mean, I knew I said we were cool, but he showed up at "booty call" hours, and I wasn't even on that. Plus, he knew damn well I didn't play about my sleep.

"Stop playing, Bambie! I got foo—"

"Well, why you ain't say that the first time?" I questioned in annoyance, cutting off Messiah as I opened the door. *This dude ain't got no shirt on,* I thought as I stared at him from head to toe. Red and black Nike gym shorts hung low on his hips as his six-pack glistened with what seemed to be sweat. The fuck was this boy doing? *You know what? Let me not. That bag looking mighty tasty though*, I mused, licking my bottom lip at the sight of the McDonald's bag.

"So, are you going to let me in or—?" Messiah spoke up, causing me to snap back into reality. I smiled.

"Of course, Binky!"

I laughed, ushering him into my apartment. Messiah scoffed.

"You's a trip, Dit—"

Before Messiah could finish his sentence, Avery's ol' extra ass waltzed out the back, looking like Luscious with that damn du-rag on.

"Mr. Ealy," he said, nodding at Messiah before grabbing the bag out of his hand and retreating back into the room like the little hermit he was. I shook my head. *What the fuck?*

"Uh uh, Daddy. Bring that back!" I shouted, trailing after him. Ain't no way in hell I was waking up at 2:00 in the morning on a school night without there being any food involved. Avery had lost his mind.

CHAPTER 30

Messiah Lafayette

"Bruh, no. Let me go!"

I laughed, pulling Bambie back against my chest as she continued to struggle to break free and go after her pops.

"Nah, Bam. Calm your ass down. I am not 'bout to allow you to walk into an ass whooping. Let that man have that food!" I spoke, trying to deter her from her seemingly set in stone "mission" to fight her daddy. It was too late and too early for me to be intervening in anybody's fight, and Dite knew her ass didn't need to be fighting Avery's ass, especially over some damn food. She was gon' fuck around and raise that man's blood pressure behind some damn McDonalds.

Her ass had better leave the man alone. I ain't come all the way over here for nothing. After giving Haley her medicine, I was left awake, feeling stupid and unsatisfied. A nigga just needed some good ol' fashioned conversation.

And some of that good ol' pu—

Nah, Siah. That ain't even you anymore.

Dite smacked her teeth, bringing me back to reality. I mentally shook my head. I had to stop thinking like that. What was wrong with me?

"Man, fuck all that! Your ass don' sat up there and woke me up out my sleep at damn near two in the morning, and for what? Nah, fuck that. I'm gon' get my food. He got the game fucked up!"

She fumed angrily, causing me to shake my head at her. She was the same ol' Dite. Don't play with her food, and she wouldn't fuck up your life.

You know what? Let me gon' ahead and nip this shit in the bud. With that being said, I opened my mouth to speak.

"Ssh... look. How 'bout I get you some more foo—?"

"That's all you had to say."

***

Looking like a whole meal out this bitch.

"Dang, you sho'nuff staring hard!" Dite joked, before slipping the straw to her punch flavored large cup of lemonade between those plump pink lips of hers as she sat across from me at the Steak 'N' Shake down the road from her house.

233

Lord have mercy. What I wouldn't give to be that stra—Nah. Siah. Stop!

"So, what brings you to my side of town?" she quizzed curiously, giving me that wide-eyed look of hers that reminded me of how she got her nickname, my Bambie.

"Hello?"

Damn, I silently cursed before clearing my throat.

"My fault. But to be honest, I just wanted to converse with my best friend. You know we don't really be talking like that. A nigga be wanting to hang sometimes," I spoke sincerely, low key eyeing her up as she ate some of her fries. Same ol' Dite. She didn't give a fuck how she ate in front of a nigga. That's why I respected her so much. See, Haley was on some dainty shit, trying to be all cute and shit when she ate, like you were supposed to look cute when you eat a burger or some shit. I mean, I loved her, but sometimes, she'd be on that extra shit. A nigga needed some chill. With Bambie, I got that.

"So what's up with you though? Ain't you supposed to be Haley's best friend or some shit? Where your ass been at for this wedding shit?" I asked. Dite laughed.

"Yeah. I thought that too."

She paused and slightly rolled her eyes.

234

"But, nah, I think her and that lil' white bitch got it all down. I ain't mad though. Hope the reception is good though," she answered with a shrug.

"I see you don't like Mariah's ass either. What's funny is that Haley barely knows that girl. She knew that bitch for like four months."

Dite hummed.

"Like I said, I hope the reception is good. Haley is still my girl, but between you and me, she ain't the same anymore. If she prefers Malibu Barbie over me, then so be it. She can have the best friend title," she stated nonchalantly. I shook my head. I see she noticed it too. Haley's ass was just always fucking shit up, wasn't she?

Dite kissed her teeth before saying, "I ain't even trying to get into all that. What's up with you?"

"I'm coolin'. A nigga ain't been working, so I've pretty much been coolin' it with my niggas."

"So basically, you've been getting it popping with Palmela." Dite joked and laughed like it was the funniest shit ever, with her extra lame ass. I mugged her.

"Nah, none of that! So how you and your dude?"

I mean, since she asked 'bout my situation, it was only fair that I asked her about hers, right?

She smiled. "We're good. Just vibing. We don't really see each other that much, because I work, and he has class and work, so..." she spoke. See, I would've made time for my girl. *The fuck you get into a relationship for if y'all don't even talk outside of the phone? I always made time for my Dite.*

Well, she ain't your Dite no more.

Aphrodite Samuels

"Oh, he good to you?" Messiah asked, although I doubted he cared about me and Derrick's relationship.

"Yeah. Like I said, we're good. We've been taking it slow," I spoke with a slight smile on my face at the thought of Derrick. The few months I've spent with Derrick were like a breath of fresh air. Derrick was a good man, and after what I'd experienced in my past, I needed that, a good man.

"Aww, I see you. You really like ol' boy?" Siah asked, and if I didn't know any better, I could've sworn I heard the slightest twinge of jealousy in his voice, but like I said, I knew better.

Bitch better have my money! Bitch better have my money! Bitch better have my, bitch better have my—.

Rolling my eyes, I immediately whipped out my phone and answered it without paying much attention to the caller ID.

"Hello, this is Aphrodite Samuels speaking. How may I help you?" I spoke into the receiver. I could hear some shuffling from the other end as I waited for someone to answer.

"Aye, I got some more fries left. You want 'em?"

Goddamn Avery.

237

CHAPTER 31

Messiah Lafayette

"So, did you have fun?"

Oh my God. I smacked my teeth as I clutched my chest a lil'. *A nigga damn near shitted on himself.* I thought, slightly mugging Haley's ass as she sat in the kitchen drinking coffee and looking like she was my mama or some shit. She had that "so where have you been" type shit going on. I smacked my teeth. *Lord, I ain't even got time for this shit.* A nigga's belly was full, mind was clear, and all I was trying to do now was take my ass to sleep so that I could get up in a lil' bit and then deal with her ass.

"Who was it this time? Trey? Or that other bitch you have been down here fucking with."

I shook my head. "Don't even come for me, Haley. I ain't even trying to hear your shit right now. Can we do this in the morning?"

I sighed in exasperation. Her ass stayed killing my high, like could I breathe for a minute before your ass start bitching? She just made my balls itch, man.

Haley laughed. Now any man in my situation would know ain't shit funny to her. Her ass was probably two seconds away from going off on my ass. Lord Jesus, give me the strength.

"Question. Do I look like boo boo the fool? Why do you feel the need to the lie to me? Just tell me who she is! Don't make me have to find out where that bitch stays."

Lord, have mercy. This woman was crazy for real.

"Look. All I'm gon' say is I love you. Now let me sleep."

With that, I went to walk away. *Lord, please keep these women from doing anything crazy. I am not trying to catch a case behind this mess, man.* I breathed lowly, making sure to keep one eye in the direction I wanted to go in and one on Haley's crazy ass. If this girl jumped on me, it was a wrap. I wasn't one for hitting females, but I'd sure enough snatch her ass up real quick if she thought she was gon' hit me and that I was just gon' take that. I was a grown ass man. I wasn't no damn child! The fuck she had going on?

I watched Haley's ass hop up quick as shit before jumping in front me. On me, this woman swore she couldn't be touched. She was lucky I caught myself. I shook my head.

"Bruh, move!" I snapped, trying to push her out of my way. I swear, I was 'bout five seconds away from catching a case up in this bitch.

"Messiah, if you're cheating on me, you need to tell me!"

Bruh, I thought, smacking my teeth.

"Ain't nobody cheating on you, damn!"

"So where your ass was at?"

I sighed.

"Steak 'N' Shake. I was hungry. You know we ain't got shit in here to eat," I spoke. I mean, I wasn't lying, but then again, I wasn't telling her the whole truth. Did she really have to know I went to go see Dite first? I think not.

Haley twisted her lips up, giving me that stank look as she crossed her arms over her chest as if she didn't believe me.

"Oh really? So why couldn't you say that earlier?" she asked. She slightly sized me up as she shook her head. I smacked my teeth. She always thought somebody was lying. *What the hell I got to lie for?*

"I'm not even trying to get into this shit with you, aight! Can I get some sleep damn? You always in my ear with that cheating shit. Ain't nobody cheating on you. I'm

240

just trying not to be all up under you. I'm a grown ass man. The fuck you got going on?" I snapped, giving her a strong ass push to the side, causing her to hit the island.

Fuck!

Aphrodite Samuels

"Mmm... I thought your ass didn't want 'em."

My daddy smirked as he watched me scoff down the leftover fries he had. I mean, what could I say? I was hungry.

Girl, you always hungry.

Okay an—girl, stop talking to yourself!

I coughed to clear my throat as I gave a mental eye roll. I had to stop doing that shit! It couldn't be normal to talk to yourself as much as I did.

"Whatever, Avery. I'm just hungry. Now leave me alone. Gon' 'bout your business."

I shooed him with a simple flick of the wrist.

"Girl, don't get slick. You lucky I'm tired."

With that being said, he left. Speaking of being tired. Let me take my ass to sleep. I knew I had shit to do in the morning. Sighing, I went to throw away the McDonalds trash before making my way to the living room.

Bitch better have my money! Bitch better have my money! Bitch better have my, bitch better have my—

Goddamn, Riri!

"Aphrodite—"

"Yo, Dite. Come get your girl! I'm 'bout two and a half seconds away from putting my hands on her."

242

I took the phone away from my ear and looked at. Lord, it was too early for this mess. Damn, Messiah. I smacked my teeth before placing my phone back up to my ear.

"Put me on speaker."

"Wh—"

"Don't even say nothing to me, boy. Just do as I say!" I demanded, and not even seconds later, I heard Messiah say, "Dite on speaker. She wanna speak to you."

"Why the fuck you call Dite?" I heard Haley yell, causing me to roll my eyes.

"Haley, baby, I'm gon' need you to calm that ass down, and listen to me."

"With all due respect, Dee, this do—"

"Yes the hell it does!" I spoke, cutting Haley off.

"If y'all ass calling me at this time in the mothafucking morning, then it does concern me. Now, what is the damn problem?" I spoke in a non-bullshitting tone. I could hear Haley smack her teeth before responding.

"This nigga out here cheating on me! He got the smell of some bitch all over him."

Bruh, I was just with this dude. The fuck was she talking 'bout?

243

I thought about it for a minute before realizing who she was talking about. Rolling my eyes, I opened my mouth and said, "Do you know this for sure, or are you assuming? Because if your ass got this man calling me at these ungodly hours over some assumptions, then we gon' fight. You know how I am 'bout my sleep. I ain't got time for this bullshit!"

Haley huffed.

"Well nobody told him to call you," she spoke, voice dripping with attitude. *I know this bitch did not... ooh, Dite, just keep your cool.* I inhaled deeply while I counted down from ten to calm myself before responding.

"Well, he did, so like I said, if you're assuming and don't have any valid proof, I suggest you take a breather and calm your ass down! The man loves you, and if he's good to you, stop expecting the worst from him. I mean, you do love him, right?"

It took Haley a few moments to respond, but eventually, she did.

"Yes, bu—"

"No buts! Love your man, and leave me alone."

With that being said, I hung up the phone before turning it completely off and placing it on the charger. *Let me take my ass to sleep.*

244

CHAPTER 32

<u>Aphrodite Samuels</u>

I walked into my home around four in the afternoon after a long day of work and was immediately greeted by the wonderful smell of sweet potato pie. *Ooh, Daddy don' made his yams,* I thought, grinning widely. Although my daddy couldn't cook much worth a damn, he sure enough could whip up a delicious pot of candied yams, and he usually paired that up with one of those roasted pork meals from Publix with the gravy. Boy! I'm trying to tell you. And I didn't want to cook today too. *Sweet baby Jesus, Avery don' came through for me!*

I grinned widely as I giddily skipped into the kitchen. As I got closer to the kitchen, I could hear my dad talking.

"Nah, you good, folk. But don't be messing' around on my baby." I heard Avery's ol' loudmouth self say as I got closer to the kitchen. I frowned. *Wayment.*

I quickly busted up in the kitchen to find my dad and Derrick conversing over a pot of gravy. *Well, ain't this 'bout a bitch?* If these dudes ain't looking like two golden girls, just sitting up here spilling all the tea like they were the best of friends. And I knew damn well they were not in here talking 'bout me.

245

"Mmm hmm, what's going on here?" I asked, gesturing between the two of them as I slipped off my shoes and tossed my keys on the counter.

"What's up, my goddess?"

"What it do, pimping?"

Both my dad and Derrick greeted me simultaneously before looking at one another.

"What kind of what, so you call big pimping, goddess?" Avery's ol' aggravating ass asked Derrick, causing me to roll my eyes at the "big pimping" part. Just childish!

"Daddy, stop it."

I laughed as I sat on one of the black stools that sat against my kitchen island.

"So, please tell me what is going on here? Why y'all in my kitchen all booed up?" I questioned curiously as my eyes darted from my dad and back to Derrick. I mean, wasn't it a bit too early for meeting the Parents' Day in our relationship? Now, I may have seemed calm on the outside, but on the inside, I was shaking. That meet the parents shit was no joke. Messiah had never officially met my dad in that way, but he did meet him, and it kind of solidified my feelings for him because my dad was my everything, and if you met Dad and he didn't call you a

246

bitch nigga, then that was a wrap. As for Omar, well let's just say my dad didn't want to meet him. Apparently, all the shit I'd told him about our relationship made Omar seem like a bitch nigga, and Avery didn't like that. Hopefully, Derrick didn't do anything stupid.

"First of all, little girl, don't nobody want your man! But you ain't tell me he could burn," Avery spoke, astonished as he referred to Derrick's cooking skills. *Wayment*!

"So you can cook?" I questioned, giving my attention to Derrick. He smirked and shrugged a little, causing me to bite my bottom lip. Ooh, this man was blessed, looking like a snack.

"Umm, lil' girl, you know I'm still in here, right? Ol' fast ass!" Avery broke out, shaking his head at me. I blushed.

"Stop it, Daddy!"

"Uh uh, don't call me Daddy! You probably call Columbus Short over there Daddy too. Yeah, I know how y'all young'ns operate."

Oh Lord.

"Avery, don't do me!"

"Shouldn't you be saying that to Columbus… no, Christopher? Any who, your man don' made fried chicken

247

and collards, and you already know I came through with the yams and gravy!"

Avery smirked, looking down at the pot of gravy. I looked around in search of the so-called fried chicken and collards. I saw the pot of greens, but that Chicken though...

"The chicken in the oven, fatty."

Daddy smacked his teeth. I cut my eyes at him.

"Anyway, why are y'all in my kitchen messing up my dish—"

Knock! Knock!

"Get the door chil'."

Avery shooed me, waving his hand dismissively. *The hell*? I stared, perplexed.

"Dadd—" I started.

"Where's my bel—"

Without giving him a chance to finish his sentence, I immediately hopped up and headed toward the front door.

Bitched up in my own home.

Knock! Knock! Knock!

The banging on the door continued, causing me to let out a frustrated groan. These niggas here! I swear, it was like people had no life these days, always banging on my door and shit.

"Bruh, wh—"

Oh my mother-loving God.

CHAPTER 33

Aphrodite Samuels

"Oh, so you're Dite's friend?" I could hear Haley ask to whom I assumed to be Samantha. I shook my head but said nothing as I continued to stare at messy Avery. I glared daggers at his ass as I watched him smile and converse with Derrick. This man had really lost his mind, swear. Not only did he invite Derrick to my house without my permission, but he had also invited Samantha, Haley, and her man who had been low key eyeing me for the longest as well. Now, Samantha, I didn't mind, and Binky was cool, but that Haley? Just because I agreed to be her maid of honor did not give her the okay to come to my house. I didn't want this broad knowing where I stayed. *Damn you, Avery*!

A chuckle from my right brought me out of my thoughts.

"Nah, that's her man. I'm her friend," Samantha said, putting emphasis on the word friend in response to Haley's previous question.

"Speaking of friend… Dite, bae, you good?" Sammy asked worriedly, shifting her once heated gaze to me. I shrugged.

"I'm good. Can you pass me them greens though?" I questioned. I wasn't even gon' let this shit get to me. I mean, we were all friends. It shouldn't be awkward, right? Maybe I was just overdoing it.

"Here. Just say the word, and I'll make her ass go ghost," Sam whispered as she passed me the collard greens bowl. I laughed at Samantha's thug-like antics. I knew one thing I could always count on was for Sam to come through with a good laugh or two. I opened my mouth to respond, but before I could, Avery's old ass spoke up instead.

"So, pimping, did you introduce your man to Beetlejuice and Michael Ealy?"

Beetlejuice? By now, Samantha and I were both rolling. This man had called this chick Beetlejuice!

"Avery, your ass a trip, talking 'bout some damn Beetlejuice!" Sam cackled, practically falling all over me at the point as tears streamed down her face. I laughed some more and looked to see Derrick smiling a little at me. Being the child that I was, I stuck my tongue out at him, and in return, he gave me that signature panty-dropper smile of his as he slipped his bottom lip between his pearly whites.

Oh, Lord. I blushed, quickly looking away. My eyes zeroed in on Messiah, and I could've sworn he was mugging me. I frowned. I mouthed "what's up" to him but rolled my eyes once he hit me with a shrug. *That boy and his problems, but that ain't any of my business though.*

"Haha, real funny, Mr. Samuels." Haley's salty ass laughed, giving off one of those butt-hurt fake laughs, causing Samantha to howl with laughter.

"Hurt bae!"

She chortled. I giggled and cleared my throat.

"No, Daddy, but this is Derrick, my—"

I paused, trying to figure out if I should introduce him as my boyfriend or not. I mean, I knew we'd said we were together, but I didn't know.

"Her boyfriend." Derrick spoke up before I could speak. I let out a breath and smiled softly.

"Anyway, girl, like I was saying, I'm saying I'm Sam, Aphro's sister from another Mister. Now everybody know each other. Aye, Beetlejuice can you pass me the yams?"

***

252

Messiah Lafayette

Haley needed to bring her ass! A nigga was ready to
go. I sighed, running a hand over my face. It was
probably nine at night, and that Samantha chick had left.
Avery had gone to sleep, leaving Haley and me along
with that nigga and my Bambie to clean up. I wasn't
trying to be in the kitchen with them niggas while ol'
lame ass tried that played out game on my best friend, so
I stepped out.

"I can't believe that nigga called me Beetlejuice! Dite
needs to check her daddy before he gets his feelings
hurt," Hurt ba— I mean, Haley whispered to me as she
plopped down next to me on Dite's sofa. I kissed my
teeth. Ugh, damn. Could I get a break? First, this lame,
and now I had to hear Haley's crybaby ass complain 'bout
some damn Beetlejuice. I shook my head. Why was I
even tripping?

You're jealous, my inner demon spoke up causing me
to shake my head in disagreement. I ain't jealous.

"So, what you think 'bout Dite's man?"

Did this broad really just—and why the fuck did she
ask like that, like she was expecting me to go into detail
'bout this nigga? Man, fuck that nigga! I coughed,
shrugging.

253

"He cool..." I trailed off nonchalantly. If she expected me to say anything else, she had another thing coming. If Aphrodite liked it, then by all means, go for it.

"Oh, that's good to hear. Then he can come to our wedding."

Wayment! I know damn well…

"What you mean he can come to our wedding?"

Haley cut her eyes at me.

"I ain't your child! Stop talking to me like that. Don' lost your mind."

I stared at her like she was crazy. She didn't even know this dude. How did she know Dite and him were even serious?

"Why you invited a nigga we barely know?" I challenged. I didn't want anybody sitting at my table if I didn't know him or didn't fuck with him! I watched Haley roll her eyes, and it took everything in me not to reach over and smack them shits out her head.

"Well, he's Dite's boyfriend. I mean, why not? You got a problem with him or something?" she retaliated.

There she goes, fishing again. I shook my head.

"Nah, invite whoever you want. Can we go now?" I stated, and without giving her a chance to speak, I left.

CHAPTER 34

<u>Messiah Lafayette</u>

I couldn't believe Bambie's ass. Like really? That lil' nigga? He wasn't shit!

Oh, so we mad now, that fuck ass nigga, Clarence, said. I frowned. Damn, my ass had gotten so damn crazy that I'd fucked around and named my conscience. On my mama, this Georgia heat had me acting all types of stupid as fuck, had me out here losing my mind and shit on some dumb shit.

Nigga, don't blame it on the heat. We all know the truth. I smacked my teeth. *Ain't nobody even thinking 'bout that girl.* I shook. Let me stop thinking 'bout shit. Fuck Clarence and that nigga, Derrick! With that thought in mind, I turned my nigga Kendrick up.

Girl, I can buy your ass the world with my paystub

Ooh that pussy good, won't you sit it on my taste buds.

I nodded my head to the beat, and I breathed lowly to control my emotions. I was no bitch nigga, and that wasn't my business who my Bambie was with, so let me stop stressing. She was doing her, and I was happy for her. She deserved happiness and nothing but.

Keep telling yourself that, my nigga. Bruh, I know damn well…

My thoughts trailed off as I mugged Haley from my peripheral in the passenger seat. I'd forgotten her ass was even in here. Her ass was mad quiet. I guess now her ass wanted to talk.

This woman here. I sighed.

"Why your ass turned down my shit?" I growled, causing Haley to give me that stank ass face she be giving when she caught an attitude.

"First of all, you ain't got to be nasty, but how was your day?" She spoke, rolling her eyes.

I frowned. "Really, Haley? I ain't working, and you ain't never home, so how you think my day went?"

Haley smacked her teeth.

"You really don't have to catch an attitude. I just wanted to talk to you, but since you want to be mad, fuck I——"

Before she could get the rest of her sentence out, I had already turned the volume back up just as Fredo Santana yelled, "Fuck these bitches! Let's get money!"

I breathed heavily. If only I had heard this shit earlier…

***

"Hey, Daddy. You want a drink?" a girl wearing red lingerie asked as soon as I got into Club Envy, a club Safari found. I nodded, took a glass from her tray, and winked at her. She walked off, swaying her hips. I stared, slipping my bottom lip in between my teeth as I watched her walk away. Her ass was nice, round, and fat just the same as her titties. She was just the way I liked 'em.

Nodding, I took a sip of my drink and winced a lil'. Cherry Vodka mixed with Red Bull. I hummed silently. I walked to the VIP section and saw Trey and them. I gave a heads up to the guy, and he pulled back the red rope.

"What's up, you boys?" I spoke, slapping hands with Trey and the rest of them niggas, bypassing Haley's dumb ass cousin. I swear, I didn't like that nigga. Who the hell had even invited his duck ass?

"Wow, cousin. So you just gon' act like a nigga don't exist?" ol' dumb ass joked like he was hurt or something. I smacked my teeth. *Man. I ain't got time for this shit. This nigga better leave me the fuck alone before I punch his ass in his neck, on God.* Deciding to ignore him, I finished my drink and put it down, watching the girls in front of me.

"Aight, Messiah, or should I say Binky? How was that lil' dinner thing, anyway? Haley told me about it."
257

I smacked my teeth. I knew damn well this nigga did not just ask that shit. On me, I was 'bout two and a half seconds away from catching thirty-eight.

"Oh, you and ol' girl went to dinner?" Safari asked, causing me to give him that Rashaad from *ATL* nod.

"It wasn't even like that. Her daddy was there, Haley, Sam, and some nigga named Drake or something."

I shrugged.

"Oooh, Juicy Fruit got a whole nigga out this bitch? Damn, if I wasn't with Tomi——"

"What, nigga? If you weren't with Tomi, what your lil' ass gon' do? Not a damn thing!" I snapped before he could finish his sentence. I grabbed one of the many Henny shots on the table and tossed that shit back before getting up and heading into the crowd of bodies.

***

"I almost decked that nigga, swear to God!" Landon ol' lying ass lied as he downed another shot of patron. I smacked my teeth. *If this nigga don't.* Ol' scrawny ass was talking 'bout some "that nigga stepped on my shoes, so you know I had to deck him". That nigga knew damn well he wasn't gon' bust a grape.

"Man, sit yo' dumb ass down!" Trey told that chicken nugget ass nigga. Lil' dumb ass quickly sat his ass right

258

down, causing me to bust out laughing. This was like some Cole and Martin shit, bruh.

"Anyway, what's up, my nigga? Why you quiet?" he asked, turning to me as he shuffled cards. After leaving the club, our overgrown asses decided to play goldfish and smoke. Now that didn't even sound right, but shit, it was whatever.

"Now Sy, my dude, what's up?" I heard Trey say, followed by teeth smacking.

"Why you always asking if Sasquatch okay? Why you don't ever ask 'bout me or them other niggas?" lil' dumb ass slurred. Now it was my turn to smack my teeth. This lil' bitch better sit his ass down somewhere. I low key mugged him as I gulped down this Henny I was babysitting. Matter of fact, I don't even got time for this shit. *Let me slide up out this bitch.*

"Sy, where your ass going?"

Shrugging, I ignored Quinton's sloppy drunk ass and stumbled out.

Aphrodite Samuels

"Shit!" I mumbled, rubbing my free hand up and down my thighs to bring warmth to them as I used the other one to change the temperature of the thermostat from sixty-four to seventy-eight. Damn, I'd be glad when Avery left. I mean, I loved my dad, but I missed my nice warm and comfy bed. It was too cold and uncomfortable to be sleeping on this couch every night.

I smacked my teeth. *Goddamn, Avery!*

"Ugh, now I'm hungry."

Rolling my eyes, I grudgingly made my way into the kitchen to fix me a plate of yams and chicken. I swear these yams were the only thing that was good 'bout my dad's visit. Not really, but really. I still couldn't get over the fact that his messy ass had all those people in my house like he paid the bills. Shaking my head, I pulled out the leftover yam and chicken bowl before getting a plate and serving spoon to help myself to some good old-fashioned leftovers.

I began to hum the melody of the food, food, food song by The Wiggles as I placed my full plate in the microwave. I maneuvered my fingers around the keypad thingy and pressed one and let it go for a minute.

Boom! Smack! Boom! Boom! Smack!

260

Who in the blue Haven? I knew damn well nobody was making a beat on my door at fucking three in the morning. Lord Jesus, somebody better be dying. I didn't have time for this shit, man. I huffed out an annoyed breath before making that long, treacherous journey to answer the door.

"Who is it!" I yelled to the other side. I heard the sound of mumbling before hearing.

"M-m-meee. It's me. B-Bambie.."

That fuck nigga, Messiah, stuttered from the other side of the door. All I could think was that this man was drunk. I sighed. Where the fuck was Haley? *Shouldn't she be keeping an eye on her man*? I frowned. I was sick of this shit! Shrugging, I unlocked the top and bottom lock and opened the door to be greeted by a giggling, barely standing Messiah Arius Zahir Lafayette.

Oh boy. I mused with a slight eye roll.

"Bambie!" ol' dumb as cheered before drunkenly engulfing me in a bear hug. Ugh, this man stunk, smelling like loud, Hennessy, and stripper booty! He sloppily began to place kisses all over my face, causing my expression to immediately morph into one of disgust at the smell of his breath. *Uh, why me? I can't deal with this man. I can't stand drunkenness.* I was all for a good time

261

here and there, but don't get pissy drunk on me. That shit was so unattractive and just flat out dumb. I drank, but I didn't get too drunk. I liked to be tipsy but not incompetent. I really couldn't believe this dude, and it was funny that he was pissy drunk because Messiah was not that type. He could hold his liquor really well, but I guess that the combination with the effects of weed was what had him like this.

"I miss you so, so much!" Messiah voiced. Nodding my head, I pulled him into my apartment before closing and locking the door.

"Go sit on the couch, Messiah!" I ordered, slightly pushing him off of me. Smacking his teeth, Messiah latched onto me even more and pulled me along with him.

"Come lay with me, Bambie," ol' stupid slurred. Sighing, I complied.

"Aight, Binky. Why are you here? Where's Haley?"

Messiah smacked his teeth at the mention of Haley's name and casually shrugged.

"The hell if I know!"

He laughed softly. Lord Jesus, give me the strength.

"I ain't got time for this." I mumbled and pushed Messiah's hand off of my chest.

262

"Go to sleep, Messiah," I spoke, fixin' to get up but was pulled back by Messiah's intoxicated, yet still strong for no reason ass.

"I love you, Bambie."

Messiah sighed against my neck as if he was inhaling my scent. Cheese and rice, man. Cheese and mothafucking rice! *I just can't.*

"Go to sleep, Messiah!" I whispered harshly to the big Winnie The Pooh man baby. He smacked his teeth but complied, causing me to let off a relieved breath. Finally! Frowning, I nestled deeper into the couch, crossing my arms over my chest, and closing my eyes. *Let me try to get another three hours in before getting ready for work,* I told myself mutely.

Silence fell across the room until, "You know it should've been you?"

My eyes immediately popped open.

"What you talking 'bout, Messiah?" I asked, but unfortunately, all I was met with was Siah's soft breathing. He was asleep. *Fuck!* Rolling my eyes, I pushed him off of me and watched the big dumbass snore softly. *Just, ugh!* I'd never wanted to punch somebody so bad until now. First, this dude came to my house late at night on some drunk shit, and then he just had to say that

263

cryptic shit. *It should've been you*. Like, what did that even mean?

Really, nigga?

I groaned. Jesus, not now. I was not trying to get into it with myself. I was already crazy enough as it is. I had to stop having these inner dilemmas.

Stop playing yourself, Dite. Deep down, you know what that shit means. Think about it!

I sighed. Did I know what he meant? How could I? I hadn't spoken to him in years. That phrase could have meant anything, right? 'Cause I knew he was not talking 'bout being his fiancée. I mean, could he? He didn't love me, at least not like that. Did I want him to? No, I couldn't. I shouldn't. I had Derrick, and I really liked him. I couldn't place myself in that what if box with Messiah. I shook my head. I couldn't go back. I was happy and content now. With that thought in mind, I slowly pushed the thought into that deep dark room in my head before letting sleep overtake me.

CHAPTER 36

Messiah Lafayette

You know that feeling that you get when you know someone's in front of you, but your eyes closed? That's the feeling I had right now, and whoever it was smelled good as fuck! I sniffed. Cherry blossoms and honey. Was that my Bambie?

Groaning, I cautiously opened my eyes to be met with two big high yella pillows. Lord have mercy. I breathed in the scent, smelling the hints of baby lotion from her breast. I knew she was my best friend, but I was a man, and they were just in my face like that. I wasn't gon' kiss 'em, but damn. A nigga could dream, right?

I coughed, alerting Dite that I was awake, causing her to immediately back away from me.

"Don't do that. Your breath flamed the fuck out of my nose!" she joked, giggling a lil' as she looked at me. Kissing my teeth, I mugged her. Oh, I see she had jokes now. That shit wasn't even funny.

I smacked my teeth, eyeing Dite. Damn, I thought. She had a pretty ass smile. Why were her teeth so damn perfect? I stared closely at her perfectly plump pink lips as she smiled and grinned, showcasing that Colgate smile as she talked. My best friend was just so damn beautiful!

265

Really, nigga, Clarence's ol' hating ass spoke up. That nigga just wouldn't let me be great. As my conscience, wasn't he supposed to support a nigga?

Think again, nigga!

"Keep it down. Avery's old ass sleep. And just lock the door when you leave, okay."

Wait, what?

"Huh?"

Dite rolled her eyes and gave me a "hmm" before saying, "I said, I fixed you a plate. It's in the microwave. Drink some coffee. My dad is asleep, so be quiet, and lock my door when you leave. I have to go to work, okay?" she recited. I nodded, causing her to smile.

"Great! I'll see you when I see you!" she spoke before hopping up off the coffee table. It was then that I took in what she had on. *What kind of teacher?* Her thick thighs filled out that green tank top dress she had on perfectly, making sure to hug every curve she had. I subconsciously licked my lips.

"Damn."

Dite smacked her teeth.

"Bye!" she spoke, rolling her eyes before leaving. I stared. *Damn, that ass though.*

***

266

"So, Dite called me. Would you care to explain yourself?"

There she went again... fishing. I smacked my teeth, tossed my keys on the table, and took off my jacket. Shaking my head, I sighed.

"I'm tired, okay? I had a long day at work. I got shot at."

I quoted Marlon Wayans in *White Chicks* sluggishly as I staggered into our room. I was fixin' to take me a mean ass nap, and Haley's ass better miss me with all that rah-rah shit. Without even kicking off my shoes, I laid down on this big ass California king sized bed and was on the edge of sleep before Haley's ol' aggravating ass just had to waltz her ass into the room.

I felt the bed dip before her fingers were running up and down my back. *Lord, please keep this woman sane.* I heard Haley sigh, and I could tell she was aggravated, but I didn't give a fuck. I didn't do shit, so I was not gon' stress her low key accusations. I was no damn cheater!

"Look, I don't know what you and your boys were doing last night, and I don't care. I just hope you used protection and that it wasn't with Di—"

I kissed my teeth, cutting off Haley as she was spitting some bullshit.

267

"For the last time. Haley, I ain't do shit, and I especially wouldn't do shit with Dite. I ain't that nigga." I voiced, tiredly. I was really not in the mood to go back and forth with this woman. I didn't even understand why she was so jealous. I mean, Haley wasn't the type to be jealous. She thought so highly of herself that you couldn't tell her anything. Now it seemed like since Bambie was around, she wanted to pull that jealousy shit.

"If you say so, Messiah. I see how you look at her! What do you expect me to think when you're always eyeing her up the way you do?"

Haley fumed. Blah, blah, blah was the only thing I was hearing right now. I couldn't believe her, talking 'bout she saw how I looked at her. *Ain't nobody checking for that girl. She's just my friend.*

I inhaled deeply, mentally shaking my head at the predicament I was in before slowly letting it out, "Oh, Lord. Why me?"

I kissed my teeth. Fuck my life, man.

"You know what? I tried. I'm just going to talk to Mariah. I'll leave you alone, since that's what you want."

With that, she left, causing me to let out a sigh of relief. *Finally*!

CHAPTER 37

Messiah Lafayette

Ring! Ring!

"Haley?"

Ring! Ring! Ring!

"For real, Haley? I know you hear that mothafucking door!" I said again but was met with silence. I kissed my teeth. A nigga couldn't sleep in peace, goddamn! Where the fuck was Haley's ass? Her ass was forever leaving a nigga to go hang out with that rat ass friend of hers. Shaking my head, I pulled myself up and went to go get the door.

Ring! Ring!

"Hol' up!" I shouted at the door. The bell rang again, and I sighed. These niggas were hard of hearing. I mugged the door. *Niggas these days.* This better not be Landon's ol' egg head ass. I swear, I was gon' karate chop that nigga in his neck, and that was on my mama. With one final groan of protest, I opened the door.

The fuck?

I stared, mouth practically hitting the floor at what was in front of me.

"Bambie?" I voiced, confused. I mean, I'm not saying I wasn't happy to see her. I was just confused than a

269

motherfucker. Haley wasn't here, and since when did she know where we stayed?

Really, nigga? That's what you worried 'bout?

I mentally smacked my teeth at Clarence's ol' aggravating ass and watched that bright, radiant smile of Bambie's take over her face, causing her cheeks to turn slightly pink as she looked at me.

"Hey, Binky!" she spoke in that sexy low and raspy drawl of hers. My soldier stirred. I thought about how good it would feel to have her on all fours with that ass up as I hit from the back. I bit my bottom lip. *Damn, bruh!*

"Dite?"

"That's my name. Now are you going to let me in?" she asked coyly. I nodded, stepping aside so she could get past. My hand gently swept across her right ass cheek, causing her to turn around and give me a look.

"Okay now, Binky!"

She laughed with a slight eye-roll before turning back around. I coughed, watching her hips sway from left and right as she walked further into my home. *When the hell did she change*, I asked myself mutely, seeing that the green dress she'd had on earlier was replaced by a burgundy two-piece with shorts so little that I could clearly see her perfectly cupped, tanned ass cheeks. Wasn't she supposed to be at work? Why was she wearing that shit?

"Oh, this how y'all living? This is nice!" she gushed in awe. I said nothing, because that ass was all that I was hearing right now.

"Why you still standing? Come sit down!" she spoke up, and without really giving it much thought, I complied. Dite crossed her legs, causing me to gulp.

"U-uh s-s-so what's up?" I asked nervously, watching as her shorts rode up on her, showcasing those glorious thick thighs of hers. I mentally groaned. It was taking all of me not to reach out and caress them. Lord Jesus, Allah, somebody, please help me! Dite laughed.

"Nothing. I was just in the neighborhood. I missed you, best friend."

She smiled, showcasing that Colgate smile of hers from earlier.

"So, where's wifey?" she quizzed nonchalantly. I shrugged. *Who the hell cares where her ass is? What you trying to do*, was what I wanted to say, but I refrained and said I didn't know. Bambie nodded, and before I could even blink, she was straddling me. *The fuck*? I coughed, noticing how close her breast were to my face. *The hell is going on?*

"I really, really, really missed you, Messiah," she moaned lowly before pressing her lips to mine. It ain't even take me a minute to respond. My hands traveled down her waist all the way to her ass and grasped it. *So plump, damn I missed this shit!*

"You missed it, didn't you?" she groaned in my ear as I slid her shorts to the side and released my stiff manhood from my shorts.

"Let me," she said as she seductively rose slightly and allowed me access to her warm cave. Her muscles gripped my dick as she bounced up and down like her life depended on it.

"Mmm," she moaned aloud. I picked her up and flipped her on her back, and with her legs above my shoulders, I dug into her until she started to squirt all over me.

"Fuck," I said, making sure I kept eye contact with her while still deep within.

I pounded faster as I got closer to reaching my peak until I heard, "Wake your ass up, nigga!"

I immediately jolted up at the sound of Trey. *What the fuck, bruh? You mean to tell me I was dreaming this*
272

whole entire time, like that shit wasn't real at all? I looked to my left and mugged the fuck out of them niggas. It was Trey, Quinton, Safari, and Landon's ol' egg headed ass. *Fuck ass niggas!*

"What y'all niggas want?" I growled in frustration. I was really thrashing that ass, and now a nigga just realized that shit wasn't even real. Quinton laughed.

"Damn, nigga! What Haley do now?" he joked. I kissed my teeth. *This nigga here.* Sighing, I sat up sluggishly and stretched. I winced at the sound of my back cracking.

"For real, what y'all niggas want?" I questioned again. I mean, besides Landon, they were my boys, but a nigga was just having the best damn dream ever before these damn goons decided to pop up on a nigga on some dumb shit.

"Nigga, where your ass went last night? I thought your ass was somewhere in a ditch, dead. Gon' fuck around and meet Mr. Munchity Crunchity on some Jeffery Dahmer shit!"

Ol' dumbass snickered. On Moses, this nigga was gon' get two-pieced. That nigga stayed doing some annoying shit. He knew damn well I didn't fuck with his ass like

273

that. If it wasn't for Haley, I would've been dropped his ass on his neck.

"Man, shut the fuck up!"

My nigga, I thought, giving Trey a low-key head nod. Trey shook his head at Landon before turning to me.

"You good though, Sy?" he asked. I nodded, shrugging. *Not really,* was what was on my mind, but it was whatever. I didn't know why my ass was up here dreaming 'bout Dite, but damn, did I wish I had finished that dream! That shit was getting good. I was just 'bout to plant my seed.

"Aight, get dressed though. We got some shit to do!"

CHAPTER 38

Aphrodite Samuels

"Oh my God. Haley, that's definitely the dress!" I heard, causing my head to shoot up from my phone screen. I smacked my teeth. *This bitch,* I mused silently in annoyance at Mariah no Carey's stank ass. The dress was an ivory fitted dress that flowed toward the end with a gold lace bodice. No lie, the dress was a beautiful dress, but on her, it was just overdoing it. Her petite frame didn't pair well with the design and shape of the dress.

"So... best friend, what do you think?" Haley spoke up. I looked up at her and smiled a fake, hope they believe it, smile.

"It's beautiful, Haley. I'm so happy for you!" I gushed in false excitement, causing all of them to cosign with me. I swear, it took a lot of me not to mug every last one of their asses. I mean, most of them were cool. Haley was Haley, and Mariah could still catch these hands if she wants to, but right now, I didn't have the energy to put up with this amount of fakeness. Between my counterfeit smile and trying to be supportive for Haley, I was going to go crazy in here. What's worse was that Mariah was sitting right across from me, and if I got from six to ten it was going to be over for her. She was already making me

275

mad by being Haley's "yes" bitch, and it was clear she didn't like me and vice versa. I inhaled deeply, counting down from ten before slowly letting it out.

"Ooh, girl, yes! Messiah just might shed a tear when he sees you in this."

Asia grinned widely as she analyzed Haley from top to bottom. I hummed in response, mentally shaking my head in the process. *I guess, chil'.* Haley giggled.

"You really think so?" she asked, causing me to involuntarily scoff. Coughing, I quickly looked down at my phone to play it off and laugh as if I were looking at something on my phone. I mentally shook my head. Look at me, just up here slipping and shit. Lord Jesus, I needed a drink.

Mariah's ol' dick riding ass shot me a look but quickly switched it up because she knew what a good ass whooping felt like. I mentally laughed and rolled my eyes. Why was I even here? I needed to leave before I hurt somebody because I was tired, and my patience was running thin with Haley. I mean, she was my girl, but she wasn't though. Man, I didn't know! I was trying to keep my cool with her, but sometimes, I just feel like strangling her ass.

Ooh, somebody's mad.

276

But I'm not though. I'm just tired.

Oh really? So, this ain't got nothing to do with Messiah?

I smacked my teeth. *Man, look... I ain't got time for this shit,* I voiced silently to my inner demon. I seriously could not with her. *Ain't nobody got time for Binky*! I'd been there, done that, and ain't never going back. I had me a man who was down for me, and there was no need for me to be tripping over Messiah's ol' aggravating ass. *Ugh, you know what? Let me not.* Messiah was just my friend, nothing more, nothing less. Just a friend... a friend who happened to be getting married to my "best" friend, and a friend who decided that we would remain just friends way back when. So, that's all there was for us. We were just two friends who had rekindled their seemingly broken friendship after years of being estranged.

I shook my head to clear my thoughts. Let me stop getting beside myself. With that in mind, I locked my phone and joined in with everybody in the celebration of Haley's dress choice.

"Yes, girl. You're going to look so beautiful!" the stylist lady spoke in agreement with previous statements.

"We can probably cinch the waist a little more just so it can be more fitted and alter the breast part a bit," she

277

added as she tugged the dress down. I nodded. The dress was way too loose on her skinny ass. I don't know why she had decided to get that dress. Niamey nodded.

"Yeah, girl. You might want to eat a lil' more. Put on some weight so the dress will fit better. You know… get you on that Dite regimen!" she joked and nudged my side, causing me to let out a small chuckle. Haley being Haley scoffed and rolled her eyes, ol' hating ass heifer.

"I'm not trying to get fat!" this bitch responded. I mugged the fuck out of her. The fuck was she trying to say? I knew damn well her ass hadn't just called me fat. I sucked my teeth and nodded. I see how she wanted to play it.

"Right!" Miss Yes Bitch cosigned. "I mean, not to say you don't look good, Aphrodi—"

"Whatever!" I spoke, cutting off the rest of the bullshit that Mariah was spewing from her mouth. I was not even going to get into it with them. I was too grown and too tired to deal with her mess. *Plus, ol' girl's fiancé ain't have a problem with it.* I mused, quietly laughing to myself at the thought. Asia laughed.

"Don't worry, girl. Them heifers just mad because you're thicker than a snicker! Don't nobody want Mariah's surfboard ass anyway," she said lowly to me. I

278

laughed in agreement. In all honesty, I was not even mad at what they'd said. I had come to terms with my weight, but it was the fact that Haley knew how much emotional pain I went through over my baby fat that never seemed to be going away growing up. She was lucky I was a Christian. God had just saved her life. Haley and Mariah had better start counting their blessings because the way I'd been feeling lately when it came to these two. Lord Jesus, I'd be on *First 48* before you could say "don't do it, Dite!"

CHAPTER 39

Messiah Lafayette

"Check my nigga out, y'all!" Quinton praised as he wiped me down like I was Boosie or some shit. I smirked cockily and went to pop my collar.

"Ah, shit! Sy in the all-white looking Godly, my nigga," Drake added and proceeded to Milly Rock. I chuckled. Black folks… can't live with 'em, can't live without 'em.

"Oh shit. Look!" I heard lil' dumb ass say. Immediately, all these egg headed ass niggas crowded Landon's annoying ass to look at whatever was on his iPhone 8 Plus. I smacked my teeth and shot all their asses a mug. *The fuck was so interesting,* I thought curiously. A part of me thought it was something dumb. Knowing Landon's ass, it probably was.

"Damn! Aye, Sy. Come look at this."

I mentally shook my head. *Speak of the devil.* Rolling my eyes, I pushed past all their asses and snatched Landon's phone out his hand, causing all these niggas to mug me. I shrugged before taking a look at what these fools were looking at. *Why the fuck?*

I glared down at the screen that showcased my Bambie in this yellow lingerie type shit, looking all types

280

of good, showing off those beautiful legs of hers. Who in the fuck had taken that picture, and who the fuck told her to put that shit on the gram?

"Sy, my dude, you good?" Trey questioned seriously. I clenched my jaw and nodded with a shrug.

"I'm good… great, actually. She ain't my girl. Ol' dude better get on that. She out here having all these niggas going coo-coo for cocoa puffs over this picture and shit. Fifteen thousand likes, " I mumbled, shaking my head.

"Now you got this nigga going!" Safari said before smacking ol' dumb ass in the back of his head.

"Don't know why you told that nigga to come over here." Drake added, smacking him in the head as well.

I smirked before saying, "Nah, I'm good. I'm done with Dite."

"See, he good!"

***

Aphrodite Lafayette

"I would've Chris Brown'd that hoe!" Sam shouted in response to what I told her about what Haley and Mariah

281

had said earlier. I shrugged. Truthfully, it was whatever. I was pretty much done with Haley and her sidekick. I was not about to stress over them anymore. I'd smile and participate in all the lil' marriage festivities, but I would not continue to allow this girl to make me feel any less than what I was.

"I'm not even pressed about it. Haley and Mariah can kiss my ass for all I care," I simply stated, giving another shrug. Young Dite probably would have beat their asses, but it was nothing but some words. I'd live. Them broads did not and would not faze me. I was too grown to be resorting to fighting, even if these hoes got slick out the mouth. I'd already come out of character with Mariah, and I didn't plan on doing that shit again unless I really had to. Samantha smacked her teeth.

"See, you better than me. Both of them hoes would've gotten done up," she voiced, shaking her head at me as if she was disappointed. Again, I shrugged. I couldn't resort to fighting every time someone talked shit about me, especially slick shit like what Haley and Mariah had been spitting. I mean, how would that look if a kindergarten teacher was fighting because someone made fun of her? That would be very childish and immature on my part, and the last time I checked, I was twenty-five, not five.

"I know, but I'm not for it anymore. In all honesty, I am done with this low-key tension building between Haley and me. I'm no longer concerned with Messiah and her. She got her man, and I got mine, so she can really miss me with all that," I replied, feeling mentally drained by the thought of this inner battle me and Haley were going through over who the hell knows… Messiah? I mean, yes. He was my first love and all that good shit, but he chose who he chose, and as a grown ass woman I had to suck it up and accept that shit. What's done was done was how I saw it. If Haley wanted to still fight over this man, then she was just going to be fighting by her damn self. I was done fighting. What was sad was that this broad was my best friend, my road dog, my day one, and now it was like "who the fuck is this girl, and why is she in my face?"

Rolling my eyes, I coughed before adding, "Girl, I'm just gon' eat and leave, simple as that."

Samantha laughed in response while nodding her head.

"You right. You right. Free food is the best food, ayeeeee!"

283

She smirked before getting up and twerking on me. I busted out laughing and pushed her ass off of me, causing her to fall face first on the ground.

"Aye, you good?"

I giggled as she got up with a groan while rubbing her face. Rolling her eyes, she flicked me off and limped her way into the kitchen. I scrunched up my face.

"Bitch, ain't nothing wrong with your leg. Why you limping?" I called out to her but was met with silence. I shook my head.

"But for real though, you cooking?" I asked, anxiously. My ass had been out all day on some dumb shit, and I was so hungry! Haley had our asses out here eating rabbit food, saying we all needed to be able to fit into our dresses. Like, bitch, what did I look like? Ain't nobody got time for that!

"What you want?"

That's my best friend. That's my best friend. I mused with a big ass Cheshire cat grin on my face. I low key Milly Rocked in excitement before hearing, "Sike!"

CHAPTER 40

Aphrodite Samuels

I heard stomping on the wooden floors near the kitchen, but I didn't bother looking up. It was just Avery's old self. He was probably looking for something to eat. I didn't feel like cooking tonight, so he was pretty much giving me the cold shoulder as if I gave a damn. I swear, my daddy was a trip. It was like dealing with an overgrown child. *Lord Jesus, give me the strength*, I silently prayed. Rolling my eyes, I took a sip of the Chardonnay that I was nursing in my little wine glass to quiet my mind before getting back to work.

"Khepri, girl, where my brown suede boots?"

Really, Avery? Really? And here I thought I was going to have some peace and quiet for once. That's what I got for thinking. Frowning, I paused my grading process before looking up from the stack of homework assignments I had in front of me. *The hell if I know*, was what came to mind, but I refrained because I knew I would get my ass handed to me if I did.

Rolling my eyes, I adjusted my reading glasses on my face before saying, "I don't know!"

I mean, he acted like I paid attention to where he put his things. Matter of fact, where the hell was he going?

He didn't know anybody but me, Sam, Haley, and Messiah, so who in the blue haven was my daddy going to see? *And who the hell would want him anyway, his big doo-doo head self,* I mentally joked with a smack of my teeth. *I can't with this man.*

"Khepri?"

I jumped at the sound of my dad's voice. *Goddamn, Avery!* This man would surely be the death of me. Damn you, Haley for inviting this man to MY home! I could've been grading these papers in pure melodic silence but noooooooo. Avery's ass wanted to be all up in my ear.

I swallowed back the animosity that threatened to spill from my mouth and called out, "Avery!" in response.

"Girl, why you yelling? I'm right here!" I heard, causing my head to turn to the entrance to the kitchen. There stood my dad dressed in a brown knit sweater, dark wash jeans, and his suede boots. I oohed and clapped.

"Mr. steal-your-mama is back!" I sang soulfully, causing my dad to flash his cat daddy smile. *Ugh, I can't with him. He so ugly.*

"Yo' daddy out'chea looking all types of good!"

He flexed. I rolled my eyes. Black folks were always overdoing it. Shaking my head, I gave him a look.

286

"Yeah. Okay, old man. So where are you going?" I asked curiously as I watched him dust off the imaginary dust off the front of his sweater. My daddy coughed.

"I gots me a date!"

"Aroo?"

Avery waved me off.

"Don't worry about it! Just know that I probably won't be back tonight, if you know what I mean."

He grinned widely, causing me to almost throw up in my mouth. *Just eww*! He swears we were like the best of friends. Nobody wanted to hear about their dad getting his freak on. *Ugh, just nasty*! I grimaced.

"Whatever you say, Avery. Do you!" I spoke nonchalantly with a shrug. Avery looked at me and smirked.

"Nah, that's her job."

I wrinkled my nose. The nerve!

***

Do, re, mi, fa, so
Yeah, yeah, yeah
Oh (do, re, mi, fa, so)
Yeah, yeah, yeah

Groaning, I proceeded to pat down the left side of my bed in search of my phone that was blaring the song "Do,

Re, Mi" by Black Near. All your girl was trying to do was sleep off the Nay in peace, but as we all know, that wasn't gon' happen. Coughing, I cleared my throat before sliding the green tab across the screen and answering the call.

"Aphrodite Samuels speaking. How may I help you?" I asked groggily.

"You just woke up?"

Nah, duh, I mused in annoyance at Messiah's stupid ass question. What the fuck did he want now? His ass had a whole girl. Why was he always calling me? Like damn, leave me be!

'\

I smacked my teeth. "What do you want?" I asked, sitting up in my bed.

"You alone?" he voiced, disregarding my question. I breathed slowly. *Jesus, why me?*

"Leave me alone, Binky!"

I groaned incoherently as I scratched my head sluggishly.

"Bambie, I'm being dead ass right now. I need some advice," he said, causing me to suck my teeth in frustration. *If I wasn't a Christian...* With a roll of my eyes, I reached over to grab my glasses off of the nightstand before checking the time on my phone. It read
288

2:00 am. I kissed my teeth. *A damn shame, can't get no sleep 'round here,* I mused in frustration as I puffed my cheeks in annoyance.

"Alright. Tell Dr. Dite what's wrong?" I teased sarcastically. Messiah hummed in response. I breathed in slowly while shaking my head. *This fool better come with it. I don't have time to be playing*, I thought. Sighing, I repositioned my glasses, fixin' to let him have it.

"Look, Binky. I love you and all, but I'm gon' need you to come with it. I'm tired!" I whined, causing ol' dumb ass to laugh. Mmm, I didn't see anything funny.

"Okay. Okay. Real talk, a nigga confused! Dite... I mean, I want to love her, but it's like... is it worth it—"

"Let me work it. I put my thing down, flip it, and reverse it."

I giggled, causing Messiah to smack his teeth. Coughing, I gathered myself together and put on my serious face.

"Continue," I went.

"It's like she doesn't trust me. Her ass always thinks I'm cheating on her, and you and I both know that ain't me. I mean, if she can't trust me, why we even doing this?"

I nodded, taking in all that he was saying. "I told you so" was what came to mind, but truth be told, I didn't tell him anything. I just let him run off with Haley because that's what he wanted, and all I ever wanted was for him to be happy.

The grass ain't greener on the other side. Yeah, yeah!

I mentally laughed at myself before shaking my head.

"Truthfully, I believe you need to think about what you're saying. I know this is kind of childish, but create a pros and cons chart of Haley, in regard to y'all's relationship," I spoke honestly. I mean, it really couldn't hurt.

"Look at it this way. If all the pros outweigh the cons, then you need to man the fuck up and get your woman! Y'all have been together for a good lil' minute, so why not try to make it work. You know? All I'm saying is, go with your heart. Do what's best for you."

I yawned, and with that being said, I blacked out.

CHAPTER 41

<u>Messiah Lafayette</u>

"Do what's best for you," Dite spoke, causing me to nod my head in acknowledgment. I mean, the shit sounded simple, right? But truth be told, it wasn't. As dumb as it sounded, I didn't know what was best for me. I mean, don't get me wrong. I liked my life as it was now, but for some reason, I didn't think I was where I was supposed to be as of now. It's like I had everything a normal man could want in life; a good job, good money, and a beautiful fiancée, but I don't know. In all actuality, I did not know what was best for me. I mean, I was content, but I wasn't happy. I sighed.

See, this was why I fucked with Dite. She made me actually think about shit, and I liked that. Damn, I missed her ass! I truly couldn't believe it had been four years since I'd had a real ass talk with somebody other than Trey. Other people just didn't get me like they did, and that was sad, given that I had Haley and all. But see, there was some shit I just couldn't tell Haley. It's not like I didn't trust her. It was just that I didn't think she'd get it. She didn't know the struggle. She didn't have to work a day in her life, and it seemed like anything she wanted, she got. Dite, on the other hand, knew of the pain, hard work, and dedication that was needed to make it happen for yourself. I kissed my teeth. *The fuck this got to do with my love life?*

Oh, my nigga, you know!

I coughed to pull myself out of my thoughts.

"Dite!" I called, only to be greeted by nothing but silence. *The fuck?*

"Bambie!" I called again, only to be met by more silence, causing me to shake my head in disbelief. *I know this woman did not just go to sleep on my ass.*

Zzz Zzz Zzzz…

Yep. She'd gone to sleep. I smacked my teeth and clicked the red end button on my phone before tossing it on the other side of the bed. *Damn, Dite!*

You know what I ain't even gon' trip. What I needed to do was get started on this little chart shit. I mean, shit. I might as well. It couldn't hurt, right?

Shrugging, I grabbed a piece paper, a pen, and started to put my thoughts on it. I thought about it. There was no doubt that she was beautiful. Any dude could see that. Her smile was like nothing else. Her teeth were perfectly straight, none missing, and white as hell! And don't get me started on her body. That shit was like, daaaaamn! Her skin was so soft and shit with just a hint of honey.

Boy! And her mind… I wasn't trying to sound sappy or anything, but I loved a girl who could think. You know, somebody who was well educated and well-spoken without overdoing it. And mama always told me, a woman who could make a man think was a woman who could hold a conversation, and at the end of the day, conversation was key. She was also fun, funny, and amazing!

My nigga, that don't sound like Haley.

Wait, what? Yes, it does!

Nah, my nigga. Since when was she funny?

Look… she has her moments.

When?

I mean, uhh… remember that time when…

Nah, nigga!

Bruh, the fuck was Clarence going on about? Of course I was talking about Haley. She was my girlfriend, and I loved her. The fuck?

Nigga, don't you mean fiancée, Clarence cut in. I smacked my teeth.

Ain't that what I just said?

Nah… you said girlfriend, my dude.

So? I know what I meant though!

Fuck this shit! With that, I slammed the pen and paper down before deciding that I needed a drink.

"Not that I don't love you, but my nigga, what you doing here? Do you know what time it is? It's damn near 3 o'clock in the morning!"

Trey frowned, shaking his head at me as he sized me up. I stood, slightly buzzed with a bottle of Bacardi in my hand.

"Again, my nigga! I'm starting to think your ass is an alcoholic. What Haley don' did now?" he added at the look of the bottle in my hand. Shrugging, I side stepped him and walked in.

"See, you always think a nigga in his feelings! I'm just coolin'," I replied. I laid on the chair and sighed. A nigga just might take a nap.

"Uh-uh, get'cho ass up, my dude!" he said before flipping the chair over. I kissed my teeth. Man! This dude was 'bout childish.

"Yo' ol' aggravating ass! All a nigga wanted to do what take a lil' nap or something."

"Nigga, you can do that at your house. The fuck you mean!" Trey shouted in annoyance. I shrugged. He'd be fine.

"Sy, my dude, really? Why are you here?" he questioned again. I shrugged again. The hell if knew. Why was I here? First, a nigga was drinking, and now, I was here.

"Bruh, come on now. Is it Dite?"

See, why did he have to bring my Bambie into this? Wasn't nobody thinking 'bout that girl!

"Don't give me that bullshit. You know that girl forever on your mind. Now what it is this time?"

Without even thinking about it, I reached into my wallet and took out a folded piece of paper before tossing it on the bed next to Trey.

"Nigga, the fuck is this?" he questioned in confusion as he opened it up. I shrugged while staring up at the ceiling in a daze. I was low key tired to be honest. Why was I here again?

Dite.

I frowned. I needed to stop thinking about ol' girl. Man, I was tripping! I heard a "hmm", bringing me out of my thoughts.

"What happened?" I asked, causing Trey to smack his teeth.

"Well," he started.

"This don't sound shit like Haley, but you know who it does sound like? Dite," he finished.

Coughing, I shook my head.

"Nah, that's Haley, no doubt," I reassured him, more so myself. I mean, it had to be Haley. Yeah, it had to be. I mean, I was in love with Di—Haley. Mmm hmm. I love her!

CHAPTER 42

<u>Messiah Lafayette</u>

"So you just gon' stay here all day?" Trey's ol' aggravating ass questioned for the hundredth time. I mugged him from my spot on the floor and smacked my teeth. *This nigga.*

"My dude, we got a problem?"

So, we mad now?

Nah, he mad. I'm chilling, I told myself, giving a mental shrug. Trey's ass was the one with the attitude. Shit, don't beat around the bush. If his ass wanted me gone, then I'd be gone. A nigga didn't want to be anywhere where he wasn't wanted. Trey smacked his teeth, bringing me back to reality.

"I'm just saying… we both know what it is. Now you need to man up, and get your shit together!" he spoke in exasperation. I shook my head.

"Nah, I love Haley!" I stated in opposition of Clarence and this guy who kept telling me otherwise. I mean, I loved Haley though. I couldn't love Bambie. It just wasn't right.

"How does it look if I go for her best friend?" I added, causing Trey to give me a nigga look. I frowned. What I do?

"My nigga, don't you know that you used to be all booed up with Dite way before you even so called caught feelings for Haley's ass! You know damn well you was in love with that girl then, and you damn sure know it now!" he argued. I waved my hand dismissively. Ain't no way I was in love with Hal—I mean Dite. She was just my friend! That's all she ever was going to be. That was all she ever wanted to be.

Trey shook his head. "Real talk though, what made you even get with Haley? I mean, Dite was cool, beautiful, and smart as fuck. So really, what happened?" Trey spoke up, causing my mind to immediately go blank. To be honest, I didn't know why I got with Haley. Maybe it was just the attention she was giving me. I mean, don't get me wrong. Dite was always there for a nigga, but she didn't act like she wanted me for me. It was like we were just hanging, and that's all she wanted. Man, shit! A nigga was feeling mighty used, and Haley made it known that she wanted me.

Coughing, I cleared my throat before responding.

"Honestly I didn't think she wanted me then. Her ass was so damn gorgeous back then and still is. What the hell would she have wanted with my bug eyed looking ass?" I stated with a shrug. A nigga wasn't no bitch, but I had hella insecurities. I felt like Dumbo with my big ass ears and a lil' bug with my eyes that seemed too light and too big for my face. The shit might have sounded childish, but it was whatever. I was man enough to admit my flaws. Nobody was perfect, but I felt like I had to be perfect for her... for Dite. Trey clicked his tongue.

"See, there you go putting words in that girl's mouth. Never, not once, did she say she ain't like you. Your ass started assuming and pulled away from ol' girl, and now look at your ass! Ain't your mama ever told you a closed mouth never gets fed? Should've been on your grown man and shit and asked ol' girl what it is or what it ain't, not get with her friend. The fuck kind of shit is that?" he snapped, shaking his head at me like he was that dude from the Everest commercial. *Well, damn*, I mused. I couldn't really say anything in retaliation. I mean, he wasn't wrong. I kept to myself and chose to move on because I feared rejection.

CHAPTER 43

A week later

<u>Aphrodite Samuels</u>

"Give me a kiss!"

I chuckled. reaching down to plant a small peck on Derrick's lips as he laid on my chest. staring up at me.

"And another one!"

Kiss!

"Another one!"

Kiss!

"One more!"

Kiss!

"Two more!"

Kiss! Kiss!

"Last one!"

Kiss!

"Ano—"

Before he could say another one, I cut him off by giving him another kiss.

"Aight. that's it! No more."

I giggled. watching as his bottom lip slowly poked out at me.

"But why? You know I love the peaches!" he spoke, in reference to my lips. I shook my head and said nope while making sure to pop the "P".

Rolling his eyes, he slightly mugged me before saying, "Okay!"

With that, he nestled his head in between my breast and inhaled. I hummed, running my hand through his hair, which he had been letting grow out for the past couple of months.

"You should keep your hair like this. I like it long." I spoke softly as I tugged and pulled on his teeny-weeny afro. I loved a man with a good head of hair. Not too long, not too short, but just right. That's why Messiah kept his long. He knew I liked it.

Hol' up why am I thinking 'bout Messiah?

"Aye, what's on your mind?" Derrick spoke up, causing me to shake my head.

"Nothing much. I'm just thinking about nothing," I reassured, more so me than him. I had to put the thought of Messiah out of my head, especially now that in a few days, he'd be getting married, so I'd have no choice but to move on for real this time. I knew I kept saying this shit, but I knew I had to keep saying it in order for me to believe it. I mean, I did really like Derrick, and I didn't

301

want to ruin a good relationship over something that wasn't guaranteed. I just couldn't lose myself over him again.

***

I slowly sipped on some Chardonnay as I flipped through this new teacher magazine I had received earlier today in the mail at the kitchen table. My body was physically tired, but my body wouldn't let go. For some reason, I kept going back to Messiah and then to Derrick and back to Messiah again. It's like my heart wanted to be done with Messiah, but then again, it didn't. My mind was telling me that Derrick was my one, but I didn't know, man! Damn, I felt like R. Kelly. My mind is telling me no, but my body... my body is telling me yes. I mean, I didn't want to have these feelings for Messiah, but I couldn't lie and say they weren't there anymore.

"Khepri? Girl, what you doing up?" Avery's ol' loudmouthed ass shouted, flicking on the kitchen light before going into the fridge and rummaging through it. I side eyed him as he took out some bread, ham, and cheese to make a sandwich.

"So, what's up? Whose ass I need to kick?" he added, giving me a look. I shook my head.

"It ain't even like that. I'm just thinking."

302

Honestly, I was just tired of these emotions. I wished I could have one day of freedom… freedom from my dad, Samantha, Haley, Derrick, Messiah, but most of all, myself. I hated being all emotional. It felt like ugh, and Daddy ain't raise no bitch! My dad smacked his teeth.

"You ain't got my peppers! And girl, you know I can tell when you lying. Now what it is?" he questioned again and began to make his sandwich. I cut my eyes at him. He swore he knew me. *Ugh, this man here.* Rolling my eyes, I took another sip of Nay before shaking my head. I exhaled once more. In all honesty, I didn't want to cry anymore. I was tired of crying over the same stupid thing. I just wanted to feel free from this love I had for Messiah. I wanted to allow myself to love someone else. The only way I could do that was to be real with myself. Damn! How come every time I found myself being a little happy, Messiah came back and ruined everything? I hated thinking about him, and I hated thinking about us, but like I said, those thoughts just kept coming back!

I sighed and ran my free hand over my face tiredly, to be quite honest, I hadn't been dealing with my dilemma like I should have been. I kept it all bottled up and just tried to get through the day. I guess I felt that if I didn't

303

entertain it, then I'd forget it, but Lord knows that ain't right.

"Lil' girl, is you listening?" my daddy snapped, pulling out of my thoughts. Shit, my ass forgot he was in the room.

I shook my head before replying, "Sorry, what happened?"

My dad clicked his teeth and frowned at me.

"Goddamn, Khepri. Now tell me what's wrong with my baby! Do I need to get my nigga-stomping Timbs out of storage? Let me know now!"

Thug life Avery. I smirked. Knowing my daddy, he wasn't playing. Being that I was his only child and the only good thing that Tamar ever gave him, I meant everything to him, and he'd do anything for me, even if that meant stomping a nigga or slapping a hoe. I shook my head.

"Daddy, I'm really not trying to get into all that right now. Can we please no——"

"Lil' girl, if you don't get to talking! Don't make me beat it out of you!" he threatened, causing me to wince at the thought of his old black belt coming in contact with my flesh. Although I didn't get whoopings often, I knew that a whooping from my daddy wasn't something that I'd

304

be able to hop up and walk off. He'd give my ass that old school ass whooping. Shit, that was hard to get over.

"But Dad—" I started, only to be cut off by my dad.

"Don't but daddy me. Spill it, or get old reliable. Your choice!"

Fuck! I frowned. I was stuck between a rock and a hard place. I mean, I knew he wasn't going to whoop me, but just the thought was scary. I smacked my teeth.

"Man, I'm not trying to do this shit!" I mumbled, tiredly. *But I should,* was what my mind was saying. I sighed. *Fuck, man*!

"Alright..." I trailed off with another frustrated sigh. I then went on to tell my dad everything about my current predicament. As I went on to tell him about my situation, I couldn't help but feel somewhat relieved. Everything was just coming out back to back, and it felt good. I had opened up to Sam a million times before, but I'd never felt this good about it. I guess it was true that I was a real-life Daddy's girl. My daddy just had a way of putting my mind at ease and making me feel relaxed enough to open up to him about everything without making me feel like I was being a burden. I always seemed to feel that way with Sam, and I knew that was not her fault. It was all on me.

305

I could tell my dad was listening intently to everything I was saying. He didn't utter a word. He just hummed every so often and absorbed my story.

"I honestly don't know what I am doing anymore! I feel that I am ready to move on, which is why I gave Derrick a chance, but then something happens, and I just keep getting pulled back into this teenage love thing I have for Messiah. I want to say I'm done, but I just can't. Samantha says that Messiah loves me, but I don't know. I mean, I always wanted him to love me back, but I can't want that anymore. We've both chosen our paths, and we should be done. Right?" I rushed out. Avery said nothing, causing me to eye him in anticipation of what he'd say next. *Come on now, Avery!*

After a moment or two of silence, he finally responded.

"Aight, look. Now after what you have told me, I ain't a big fan of Michael Ealy, but it's clear to everybody but you that the boy is in love with your big-headed ass! And don't get me wrong, I like Columbus Short, but it's clear to see where your heart is at. Now I don' told you, if your heart ain't all in it, then it ain't for you. The shit you got yourself into ain't right for Columbus or yourself, and you

306

know I taught you better," Avery spoke, taking a long deep breath before continuing.

"You grown, so I ain't gon' tell you what you need to do, but we both know what that is. Right?"

Coughing, I nodded meekly.

"Yeah, I know."

CHAPTER 44

<u>Aphrodite Samuels</u>

I slowly sipped on my Nay as silent tears streamed down my face. I swear, I'd become an alcoholic in these past few months, and it was kind of scary, but I didn't know what to do. My love life was so fucked up, man! It was like I'd take one step forward to take two steps back. I already knew what I had to do, but it was easier said than done. I mean, I was going to do it. I just didn't know when.

I sighed. I was going to have to end things with Derrick before shit got real. Avery was right. It wasn't fair to him, and it wasn't fair to me. He was better than this. Hell, I was better than this. I wasn't saying this would open doors for Messiah and me, but it would make things a little easier for me, hopefully.

I knew deep down that I was still hooked on Messiah, and as crazy as it may have sounded to some, I could see myself waiting for him. I mean, who knows. Maybe both my dad and Samantha were right. Messiah loved me too. And besides, if he didn't love me, I owe myself the right to some closure. I needed to know why he chose Haley and where we went wrong. Plus, it was also time that I started seeing Haley for what she truly was, a bitch.

308

Knock! Knock!

I jumped, startled by the loud banging on my door.
Who in the hell? Goddamn, Avery! He was supposed to
be gone for the whole night after he left the second time,
or at least that's what he had told me. Apparently, I
needed time to myself. Well, so much for that. I shook
my head, setting the bottle down before going to the door.

"Daddy, I—Messiah?"

I stared at Messiah. *Are you serious, G*, I mused in
slight amusement as I looked toward the sky quickly
before bringing my eyes back to Messiah.

"W-what are you doing here?" I asked, anxiously,
slightly shifting my weight from one foot to the other. I
breathed in exasperation, refraining from rolling my
sleeves up to cool myself down. It was, sure enough,
getting hot in here. I reached up, placing a hand on my
chest to try to steady my breathing. Lord Jesus, give me
the strength! I cleared my throat.

"What are you doing here?" I asked again but
stronger this time. I watched his lips form into a small
smirk, and before I could react, his body was pressed
firmly against mine, lips engulfing my own, and his
hands curiously exploring my curves.

What the fuck, was what was on my mind. It was like I was glued to his lips and him to mine. In all honesty, I didn't want to stop. I didn't want him to stop. And with that, I allowed myself to be taken away by the intoxication that is Messiah.

***

Boom! Boom! Boom!

My ears twitched at the sound of my heart that seemed to grow louder with every breath I took. I bit down hard on my bottom lip, bringing the blanket closer to me as I fought back tears. I couldn't let myself cry. I didn't deserve to cry. I knew what I'd done was wrong, and I couldn't change that. I felt shaken but immobile whilst Messiah slept peacefully next to me with his arm wrapped loosely around me.

I can't!

But you did though, was what my conscience replied, causing me to smack my teeth in exasperation. *Shut the fuck up, Dite,* I screamed back at myself. I was already feeling like shit, and I didn't need to get beside myself. I couldn't play the victim either. I told myself I wouldn't be a cheater. I was no cheater, but now, that shit had gone out the window, and the bad thing about it was that I didn't feel bad that I'd slept with Messiah. That was what

310

really scared me. To be quite honest, I'd enjoyed every bit of it. The feelings of his large hands wrapped around my body and the way he held me and took care of me over and over again last night was amazing! I didn't want to love it, but I did.

"Morning," I heard Messiah mumble gruffly against my side, causing me to look down at him.

"I love you, Bambie!" he added, tightening his grip on my hips. I said nothing. All I could do was stare in awe at him. I couldn't find the right words to say to him at the moment. A part of me wanted to overindulge with this painfully sweet essence of Messiah, but the better half of me knew this was wrong. He shouldn't have been in my bed, and I shouldn't have wanted him to stay, but he was, and I did.

I can't, man, I thought again. This man should not have been in my bed, telling me he loved me while he had a whole fiancée waiting for him at home. Not mention, I had a boyfriend. Did he not see that this was wrong? I don't know what came over me, but my shame soon morphed into anger. I was angry at myself for allowing and loving this, and I was mad at Messiah for acting so unfazed and making me feel this way. I mean, what did he take me for? A jump off? I wasn't someone he could fuck and go back to wifey. This wasn't freshmen year. He couldn't have his cake and eat it too. *I won't be his second choice*, I mused in slight determination.

With that thought in mind, I said, "I think you should leave."

Messiah's head immediately shot up. He gave me a look that screamed *the fuck*.

"Bruh, what you talking 'bout?" he questioned in vexation. I rolled my eyes.

"What I just said! Go back to Haley," I spoke sarcastically before pushing him off of me and getting up from the bed.

"Get your shit, and go!" I snapped, throwing his clothes at him.

"What the fuck, bruh?" he asked in confusion.

"Why are you doing this?" he added, getting up to grab me. I smacked my teeth. *This dude*! I smacked my teeth.

"Can you please get off of me?" I spoke as calmly as I could. What I really wanted to do was cuss his ass out and then some, but I refrained. I just wanted him out of my room, out of my home, and out of my life! Messiah shook his head, eyeing me with this intense look that made me feel flustered.

312

"I'm serious, Bambie. Why you mad?" he asked again, making sure to keep eye contact with me. I gulped. I felt like I was stuck between a rock and a hard place. I felt torn. I wanted to snatch away, but I just couldn't. I sighed.

"I-I-I just don—"

Before I could finish my sentence, I was caught off guard by Messiah's lips. Fuck!

No, no, Dite! Get your shit together! I mentally sighed.

"We can't," I mumbled against his lips.

"Yes, we can." Messiah whispered back. I groaned.

"What about Haley?"

Messiah smacked his teeth.

"I love you!"

"Like you love Haley?"

To that, Messiah smacked his teeth.

"What you trying to say?"

"I'm saying that you have a fiancée who you love! We can't be doing this."

Feeling the tears form caused me to blink them back.

"You know this ain't me. I ain't no cheater!"

"Sure, I love Haley, but I'm in love with you! You're my one," he replied, caressing my cheeks. He sighed.

313

I said nothing and just stared at him. He loves me. Deep down, I wanted to smile at that thought, but then I thought about Haley and the fact that he was still with her. *Damn.* I softly shook my head.

Before I could even say anything he asked, "You love me, right?"

"Y-ye can't. I mean, I can't. You should go!" I stuttered. Messiah searched my eyes for any sign of uncertainty.

"You sure 'bout that?"

No.

"Yes."

"You don't really mean that."

I coughed, conjuring up the courage to respond.

"No, you need to go. I can't be your second choice. Figure out what you want. Please just go!"

Messiah nodded.

"Fine."

And with that, he left. Damn, I had fucked up.

CHAPTER 45

<u>Aphrodite Samuels</u>

"Ooh, girl, it smell like all types of Fabuloso in here! It's looking mighty clean in here. Maybe I need to invite you to clean my apartment," she joked, dropping her purse on the couch and kicking off her shoes. I rolled my eyes. This chick swears she was funny. I gave a mental shrug, watching as she bypassed me and went straight to the kitchen. *Fat ass*! I shook my head. *Don't make no damn sense. I'm over here in distress, and this bitch eating up my food. Not only am I going to be depressed, but I'm also going to starve to death.*

"Okay, so what's up? What's the tea, sis?" she hollered from the kitchen. Damn, I'd almost forgotten about that.

Yeah right!

I swallowed back the shame and blinked away the tears before speaking.

"Uh-um I-I did something… with Messiah," I replied, mumbling that last part.

"You say what now?" she called. Where was that nosy ear when you needed it? I really didn't want to repeat myself, but since her ass didn't want to channel her

315

inner Rosy the nosy neighbor, I had no choice. Fuck my life!

"What's the tea?"

I heard her ask but this time closer. I blinked a few times, finally realizing that she was in the room with me. I frowned. This bitch had two ham and cheese sandwiches with a bag of chips and a cold Arizona to go with it. Shaking my head, I ran my hands through my hair, slightly scratching my scalp before responding.

"I uh… slept with Messiah."

Samantha gasped.

"Bitch, you lying!"

I shook my head.

"Girl, what happened?" she questioned in anticipation. I smacked my teeth. *This bitch.* Her ass knew she loved a good story. She lived for tea, and boy did I have some tea for her. I breathed in slowly and held for a good five seconds before letting it out.

"I was with Derrick yesterday, and I started to think about Messiah, which got me in my feelings. Then I talk to Avery, and he got me thinking about what I want. Then he came here, and one thing led to another," I summarized quickly. *The fuck is she smiling so hard for,* I thought, noticing the crazy cat lady smile she had on her face.

"One question... Was it good?"

Really, dude?

"Okay, okay, I'm sorry, but what about Derrick? Did you tell him yet?" she quizzed. I shook my head in shame. I mean, it did just happen last night, but that was no excuse.

"Well, you need to tell him."

I shook my head again.

"But I can't!" I protested. Samantha rolled her eyes.

"You gon' have to. You and I both know that ain't right, and like you always say, that's not you," she said, giving me a look. I kissed my teeth. She was acting like it was easy to tell someone some shit like this. How could you tell the person you were involved with that you were in love with someone else and that you cheated on them? I just couldn't. I wanted to, but I didn't know how! I huffed.

"I don't know how, Sam... I just don't."

"Okay, look."

She paused with a tired groan.

"I understand it's hard for you, but look. You made your bed. Now you've got to lie in it," she finished. I

317

nodded. I knew she was right. I had to own up to my shit. There was no way around it. Without saying anything else, Samantha handed me my phone while giving me that *do what you got to do* look.

***

"You good?" Derrick asked immediately once I opened the door for him. I nodded, rubbing my arms like I was a crackhead or some shit. I was nervous, and it didn't help that Samantha's ass decided to leave me to do this on my own. What if this dude went off on me? I could stick and move, but Derrick looked like he could fuck some shit up if he had to. I mentally rolled my eyes at myself. *Let me stop jumping to conclusions.*

"Goddess, are you good? You looking a little stuck," Derrick voiced, bringing me out of my thoughts. He cuffed my cheeks, looking at me with concern filled eyes.

"Be honest," he murmured, looking me up and down. Fuck! Could he not look at me like that? I already felt bad as it is, and the fact that he was looking at me with so much compassion was what made me feel worse than I already felt. *Damn you, Dite!*

"Uh, um I-I-I um… I need to tell you something," I stammered, taking his hands off my face and placing them down by his sides.

318

"I-I-I can't d-do this no more!"

"Wait a minute. What I do?"

I sighed. Here, I was supposed to say, it's not you, it's me. What type of shit was that? But this was what I get for not thinking. I mentally shook my head to clear my thoughts. It was time to woman the fuck up! *You got this*, I told myself, mentally preparing myself as if I were a Money Mayweather getting ready for a fight. I exhaled one last time before responding.

"Isleptwithmyex!" I rushed out, bracing myself for any repercussions. *Lord Jesus, don't let this man do anything crazy.* An awkward silence fell between us. I gulped.

"You know what... I ain't even..."

He shook his head, and without saying anything else, he left.

CHAPTER 46

A month later

<u>Aphrodite Samuels</u>

"Fuck!"

I dry heaved alongside my tub as I sat on the toilet. My stomach churned, and I didn't know if I needed to shit or throw up. It sucked when you wanted to throw up but you couldn't, because you might shit on yourself at the same time. Fall break had just begun, and I had basically cut all ties with Haley and Messiah. Haley, being the bitch that she was, didn't mind. That damn Messiah kept calling me, so I had to block him. I would not be his side chick, and that's on God. I smacked my teeth. Man, forget Messiah. My damn stomach was hurting, and my dad was nowhere to be found. His ass said he wasn't trying to catch Ebola fucking around with me. He'd been staying with some woman named Charlotte who he had been seeing lately. Speaking of Charlotte, I still hadn't met that lady.

I groaned, feeling the churning in my stomach start to rise. *Fuck*, I silently cursed, turning over to empty out whatever was left in my stomach into the little trash container on the side of me.

"Khepri!" I hear Avery shout from the front of the house. I groaned. Could I please be left alone? That damn Avery was always messing with somebody. I smacked my teeth, cringing as my stomach bubbled. *Why me, Lord?*

"Charlie made you some soup! Where you at?" he asked, causing me to roll my eyes. If this man didn't leave me alone! I didn't have time for his mess, and who the fuck was Charlie to be fixing me soup? I didn't know that woman, and everybody knew Aphrodite don't eat from just anybody.

"Daddy!" I groaned in pain, and not even seconds later, my daddy showed up with some gloves, a surgical mask on, and a can of Lysol disinfecting spray in one hand. I wanted to mug him, but I just didn't have the strength to.

"Damn, baby girl. You look 'bout dead!" ol' raggedy ass mumbled. I sighed. If only I could scowl. Damn, I hated being sick, and it was always around early fall to winter time, even with the flu shot.

Avery shook his head and went to spraying. I started to cough as I inhaled the spray.

"Avery! Avery! You gon' kill me!" I protested, fanning my face sluggishly to rid myself of the seemingly toxic fumes. I watched my dad shrug before lifting the mask.

"Girl, bye! Are you done shitting?" he voiced, eyeing me up and down. I kissed my teeth. *No filter.*

I rolled my eyes, or at least tried to before asking him to get me some Pepto Bismol to settle my stomach. Avery being Avery just had to make a scene as he walked back out of the bathroom talking 'bout some, "Your ass is asking for a lil' bit too much of me."

I swear he was so extra. *I can't with him.* I sneezed. "Thank you!"

Once my dad left, I wiped myself before flushing the toilet, washed my hands, and sprayed the bathroom. My stomach seemed to be settling, so I was gon' take my ass to sleep before Avery came back. Groaning, I limped out of the bathroom into my room before crawling into bed and curling into a ball under the covers.

***

"Here comes the airplane!" Avery's childish self cooed as he spoon fed me the soup. I told this man I could feed myself, but he just had to be extra. After taking a good sixty-minute nap, Avery decided I'd had enough sleep and needed to eat, so here my twenty-five-year-old ass was playing here comes the plane with my dad as if I was an infant. *Well at least somebody cares about me,* I thought weakly. Samantha's ass deserted me to go to Paris, and Derrick didn't fuck with me anymore, so there was that. Plus, I didn't really have friends to call on in the time of need. Ugh, *let me stop acting like a loner.*

Shrugging out of my thoughts, I gestured toward my cup of tea so that my dad could give it to me. Again, extra ass decided he was going to hold my cup for me as I sipped.

"Now, I put a little lemon in there too," he spoke, causing me to stale face him. *This man here.* I mentally rolled my eyes and took a sip of the tea, cringing at the overpowering lemon flavor.

"Dang! No sugar, Avery?" I wheezed. It was now Avery's turn to stale face me.

"Lil' girl, you better gon' somewhere! I'm trying to do you a favor," he stated, undermining my annoyance with him. *Ugh, Lord!*

"Daddy, I'm tired!" I whined, tiredly. All I wanted to do was go to sleep, but here I was eating. I couldn't even keep down food as it is so what was the point?

"Can I go back to sleep now?" I pleaded.

"No, you need to eat. Who told your duck ass to miss that flu shot? They were giving them shits out free, and

323

you know we Samuels don't pass up free stuff," he argued, much to my dismay. He mugged me, clearly seeing my frustration with him.

"You ain't too sick to get popped. Now get some more of this tea so that you can stop all that damn coughing. Your ass over there about to cough up a lung," he quipped, holding the teacup up to my lips. Mentally groaning, I gulped down some more of his nasty ass tea and shook my head to say no more. Avery complied and proceeded to feed me soup. After a couple more spoons full of soup, he finally stopped.

"Aight now. I don' fed you and gave you some medicine. Now you can go back to sleep."

And with that being said, he left me there alone at the kitchen table. Wait, what the fuck? I stared, perplexed, at the spot Avery had occupied before he left. I couldn't believe this man. The audacity!

"Hahaha, I'm just playing!"

This old man laughed, coming back into the room and helping me get up. I swear his ass played too much. I really thought he had abandoned me. At that thought, I started to cry. Avery groaned.

"Oh my God. Please don't."

"I'm sorry!"

I sobbed and began to wipe tears away. It wasn't uncommon for me to cry when I was sick. It just happened. I don't know why, but I did.

"I-I just… my back h-hurts!" I cried some more, knowing I was lying. I mean, it tingled, but it didn't hurt.

Avery shushed me as he patted my head in comfort as if I were a child before saying, "It's okay, Khepri. I got you."

I nodded and kept quiet for the time being.

CHAPTER 47

<u>Messiah Lafayette</u>

Trey eyed me in disbelief.

"Bruh, how your dumb ass gon' wait this long to tell me you slept with ol' girl?"

He laughed, shaking his head at me. I shrugged.

"I know, bruh. Something just told me to go see ol' girl, and shit got real," I responded. I wasn't ashamed of what happened. I was just shocked that it went that far. All a nigga wanted to do was talk, but going there and seeing her looking all sad and shit made a nigga want to take care of her. I mean, sex wasn't the answer, but still. I just wanted to make everything okay, but I guess I'd made shit worse, seeing as how she kicked my ass out. Was it bad? I knew Bambie's body like the back of my hand, and the way she was moaning said otherwise. Shit, man. I didn't know!

"Aye though. What was your ass still doing with Haley? I mean, if you and Dite hashed shit out, shouldn't your ass be with her fucking like rabbits or some shit?" he joked again, causing me to smack my teeth. *If only*.

"Nah, she kicked my ass out in the morning and ain't hit me up since," I answered, confused as to what had happened between the time we'd laid down together to that morning.

Trey hummed, nodding his head.

"Here's a thought. Maybe she was uncomfortable."

The fuck? Noticing my look, he went on.

"Look, we all know Dite is a good girl. She ain't crazy, and she wholesome. Plus, she got a man, so why wouldn't she be uncomfortable that she woke up to find you in her bed?"

Damn, I hadn't thought about it like that. Oh, shit. I remember back then she did say something 'bout her mom cheating on her pops and shit like that. Damn, I had fucked up.

"See, this why you my nigga. I need to go talk to her!" I stated, and without waiting for Trey to say something else, I left.

***

"Let me get uh… um… two number sevens, an Oreo Mcflurry, three chocolate chip cookies, and a large iced tea," I ordered. After leaving Trey's, I made my way to McDonald's to get me and Dite some food. I probably wouldn't get in if I showed up at her door empty handed. Plus, I knew she loved to eat.

327

"Will that be all, sir?" ol' girl behind the counter asked me. I ignored the look she was giving as she typed in my order. Lil' shorty was cute, and all but ol' girl looked 'bout eighteen. The fuck did I want with an eighteen-year-old when I had my Bambie anyway? Shrugging out of my thoughts, I nodded.

"Yeah," I answered in monotone. I wasn't trying to let shorty think she had a chance, and I hoped she wasn't one of those types who couldn't see when a nigga didn't want to be bothered.

"You know you kind of cute, right?"

And here it goes! I mentally smacked my teeth. If this lil' girl didn't go on somewhere. I coughed and told her thank you but didn't say nothing else as she calculated my total. After a hot a little second, she finally told me my total. I quickly handed her a fifty-dollar bill and waited for my change. Once I got my change and receipt, I stepped to the side.

"You know my name is Jaylin. What's yours?"

I smacked my teeth, bruh.

Sighing, I replied, "Messiah, and I have a wife," I spoke, dismissively. I was way too old for this lil' girl, and like I said, I had my Bambie. I didn't need anybody else. Lil' girl smacked her teeth, finally realizing I wasn't

328

having it and ignored me as she continued to do her job. I shrugged. *Be mad. I don't give a fuck,* I thought. Wasn't nobody checking for that girl anyway. You know what? They needed to hurry up with my food so that I could get to my woman.

"Order number sixteen!" I heard, causing me to raise my hand up before grabbing my food off the counter. I made sure to check the bag before leaving. After a good thirty minutes or so, I finally arrived in front of her apartment building. Without wasting anymore time, I parked my car, grabbed the food, and exited the car.

Breath good?

I cuffed my hands around my mouth and blew.

Yeah, I'm good.

Look good?

I dusted off my shoulder before smoothing down my clothes. Check!

You calm?

I shrugged and did some light breathing before nodding.

Yeah, I'm good.

And most importantly, was the food warm? I reached into the McDonalds bag and felt that the food was still warm and sighed in relief. I might have gotten my ass cussed out over some cold fries. I mentally gave myself the thumbs up before proceeding to knock on her door.

"Aye, Bambie. Open up!" I shouted but got nothing in response. I kissed my teeth. Her ass just had to be difficult. *Ain't nobody got time for this.* With that, I picked the lock. Frowning, I walked in and noticed the room smelled heavily of Lysol and incense. *The fuck?*

"Dite?" I called, shutting the door behind me. I continued to call her name as I tossed the food on the kitchen counter.

"Bambie. I brought food!" I tried but to no avail. *Fuck,* I silently cursed. Her ass was probably sleep. With that thought in mind, I went into her room. There, I saw her curled up on one edge of the bed, looking like she was about to fall off. I laughed. That's my Bambie.

"Bambie?!" I called. She didn't move. I smacked my teeth. Her ass was a heavy sleeper for sure. I guess I'd wake her up. I went over to her side and began to shake her.

"Aye. Dite. Wake up, baby. Come on!" I tried again, only to get the same result. *The fuck?* I felt her forehead and noticed how hot she was.

"Bambie! Bruh, come on!" I pleaded, trying to get her to open her eyes. Cursing, I drew back the cover and

330

noticed her blood-soaked sheets. I jumped back quick as fuck. *What the fuck! Shit, shit, shit!* I picked up the phone and immediately called the ambulance. *Damn, bruh what the fuck?*

CHAPTER 48

<u>Messiah Lafayette</u>

"You ready, my dude?" Trey asked, giving me a slight slap on the shoulder. I wasn't gon' lie. I was nervous. My palms were sweaty, face was hot as fuck, and it felt like I couldn't breathe. I couldn't believe I was about to get married in the next five minutes. Damn, a nigga wouldn't be riding solo anymore. Alright, nigga, you got this! I breathed.

"Aye, how she look?" I asked, looking toward Drake expectantly since he had been the one to have gone out to check up on the girls. She wasn't one for the whole "you can't see the bride's dress before the wedding". I mean, we were practically together the whole time up until this point, but I didn't feel it was right to see her dress before the wedding. As corny as it sounded, I wanted to be surprised when I saw her in her dress. I wanted my heart to feel like it was going to explode with love when I saw her. I just wanted my baby to shine today. It was her day, and I was just here. Don't get me wrong. I loved the fact that I was marrying this beautiful, smart, and amazing woman, but I just wanted to be married already.

"She looks like she looking. Now come on! You's 'bout to be married now, boy," Drake spoke, shaking his head at me.

"I'm happy for you, dude. You deserve this," he applauded with a nod of respect. I gave him a head nod back as to say thank you. Just then, I heard a dolphin like cackle, and I already knew who it was.

"Aye, my dude looking sharp out this bitch!" Landon's ol' loudmouthed ass shouted, coming to stand beside me as I fixed my tie in the mirror. I mugged his reflection. This nigga here!

"Real talk. I know I get on your nerves a lot. Hell, I get on my own damn nerves, but I'm really happy for you, bruh! You a good dude, and I'm happy she's going to marry someone like you," he spoke seriously, giving me a slight pat on the back as he grinned at both of our reflections. I mentally laughed. And here I thought he hadn't peeped shit. I guess I was wrong.

"You right. You do get on my nerves, but that's real what you said, man. Thanks," I replied. I then began to straighten out my jacket and sighed.

"Truth be told, maybe I am a lil' too harsh on you. You ain't all that bad," I added with a shrug. I watched *as this nigga's lips stretched from one side of his face to the other.*

"See, now we're getting somewhere!"

He grinned like the psycho he was. He then went in to hug me, but I quickly blocked him. I shook my head.

"Nah, my nigga. You good." I said, giving him that "don't touch me" look. I knew we'd just had a heart to heart and what not, but we weren't that cool. Landon laughed, holding his hands up in defense as he backed away.

"Say less, my dude."

He laughed.

"Good luck. Now let's go, y'all!" he spoke, ushering all my groomsman out the door. It was now Trey and I left.

"I can't believe it, man. Today is finally here."

I sighed, causing him to laugh.

"Yeah, I know. Thought this day would never come, but you finally getting what you've always wanted. Now you got to go out there and do your thing. You got your vows?" he questioned. I nodded.

"Yeah, I memorized them."

"Alright, let's do this shit!"

With that, we both went out to join the boys next to
the pastor. I hummed quietly to myself and watched the
flower girl line the path with pink roses as the choir we
hired started to sing softly. It seemed like a minute after
the flower girl had passed that she had finally stepped out
with her dad.

Damn!

"That's my Bam——"

"Mr. Lafayette!"

I jumped into a fighting stance and began to search
around in search of the voice. I heard a laugh. Before I
noticed, some dude in blue scrubs walked up to me.

"I'm sorry if I scared you. You can put your set down.
Everything good," he joked, laughing at the face I was
giving him. This nigga was 'bout to get his ass slumped
round here. You don't wake anybody up out their sleep
like that, and a nigga was having the best dream, I think.
It was my wedding day, and I could've sworn I was about
to say Bambie, but maybe I was wrong. Shit, I don't
know.

"Anyway, what's wrong with my wife?" I asked
bluntly. I wasn't trying to stay here and talk to this man
all day. I needed to know if my girl was okay. I breathed
in deeply. *God, please. I know I don't talk to you like*

335

that, and I ain't no saint, but please don't take my girl
away. We don' been through so much. I can't lose her
now. That's my heart right there, man. Please let her pull
through.

I silently prayed. The man smiled, and I immediately
I felt relief wash over me.

"You'll be happy to know that we were able to stop
the bleeding. Your wife had a high fever of 102, but we
were able to bring it down, and her body has been in a lot
of stress, which could have terminated the pregnancy,
bu—"

"Hol' up! Pregnancy?"

Ol' dude looked confused.

"Did you not know?"

I shook my head. *Pregnant?*

"Well, yes. Your wife is indeed pregnant, and from
what we can tell, she is six weeks along."

I let whatever else the dude was saying drown out,
and all that was on my mind was *pregnant*. How could
she be pregnant? Did she know? Who was the father?
Was I the father? All these questions clouded my head,
and I cringed. *What the fuck, bruh?* I hummed.

"When can I see her?" I asked, getting straight to the
point. I needed to know if she was holding this pregnancy
336

from me and if it was mine as soon as possible. If I was the father, then I was gon' do what I had to do. I'd always envisioned her having my kids anyway, but if I wasn't, I don't know, man. That would mean she'd had sex with me and some other nigga around the same time, and that shit wasn't right. I breathed. We'd see.

"She's actually resting as of now, but you can go see her. She's in room 613."

I thanked ol' dude for saving my girl and the baby before walking away.

CHAPTER 49

<u>Messiah Lafayette</u>

Damn. Dite. I sighed, running my hands over my face in exasperation. I looked down at Dite and shook my head. How the hell could she be pregnant? We'd only done it one time.

In the words of Migos, it only takes one time.

I shrugged my shoulders and went to touch her stomach. She moved.

"The hell?" she said in a cracked voice, and I looked at her.

"Hey, Bambie," I said with a slight smile as she looked at me in confusion. Her face was so pale, and she looked tired. *Jesus, Dite.* She coughed.

"Am I in the hospital? What happened?" she asked, looking around at the wires and machine she was hooked up to. I smacked my teeth.

"You almost had a miscarriage, Aphrodite. How come you never told me?" I asked in anger. I mean, how could she not know? Weren't there like signs and shit? She should know her own body. It was now Dite's turn to smack her teeth.

"First of all, watch who you're talking to, and what the hell you mean pregnant? I haven't been with anyone since…" she trailed off. I watched as her eyes grew wide, and her jaw hit the floor. She gulped.

"I can't," she spoke in disbelief with a shake of her head.

Wait, hol' up.

"What you trying to say? You don't want to have my baby!" I snapped in anger. How could she deny my baby? The fuck she wanted, an abortion? On Moses, she'd better not be on some dumb shit. If she killed my baby… man, don't even get me started on that. She mugged me

"Why the fuck are you mad? I didn't even say anything!"

"Nah, but you were thinking it. Weren't you?" I asked rhetorically. I already knew the answer to that. Of course she didn't want to have my baby. She wanted that lil' nigga's baby. She didn't love me. Man, fuck her!

"You know what? Fuck this shit."

I took one last look at her and shook my head. If she couldn't, then I couldn't either. I was done. With that thought, I left.

Aphrodite Samuels

"This lil' guy seems to be doing a lot better. You just have to remember to drink your fluids and take your vitamins. Some Tylenol should help with the fever. Oh, and remember to take it easy," my doctor, Dr. Sanders, recited as the ultrasound thingy glided over my stomach. I inhaled and exhaled slowly, feeling mentally drained at the fact that I was pregnant. I honestly couldn't believe it. I may have loved Messiah, but this man was engaged for crying out loud! He was going to be married, and this baby wasn't even planned. How could I bring a child into this world, knowing that I wasn't supposed to have him? This baby was supposed to be Haley's. She was his fiancée, so it was only right that she had his first child, but now shit was all fucked up.

"So, where is Mr. Lafayette?"

"Hmm?"

Dr. Sanders laughed.

"I asked where is your husband?"

Husband? What the fu—oh, Messiah.

"Uh, he had to step out for a few," I answered shortly. I couldn't believe he told these people he was my

340

husband. He'd better take that shit back to Haley. The fuck did he have going on?

Ooh, somebody's mad.

Ya damn skippy!

First, this dude had the audacity to accuse me of wanting to get an abortion, and now he was up here telling these people I was his wife like he didn't have a whole female out this bitch. I couldn't with this man.

"And he's not my husband. He's actually marrying someone else," I blurted out, mentally face palming myself. Why the hell did I tell that man that? He didn't need to know my business. Now he'd probably think I was some hoe or something.

"I didn't mean for this to happen!" I exclaimed before he could utter anything. Dr. Sanders nodded.

"I see. I'm not judging. Truth be told, that's how me and the Mrs. met. She was in a relationship, and I was, as y'all young'ns say, friend zoned. One thing led to another, but here we are twenty years strong. Look, the bottom line is that even if things aren't ideal, it doesn't make it wrong. Sooner or later, you'll find what you're looking for. God gon' make a way."

To be continued...

341

Contact info:

Email: Carlyle.Raesha@gmail.com

Instagram: @thenotorious_rae

Facebook: @GoddessLifeRae

Be sure to LIKE our Major Key Publishing

page on Facebook!

CPSIA information can be obtained
at www.ICGtesting.com
Printed in the USA
LVOW10s1505060218
565499LV00012B/793/P